Fair Annie of Old Mule Hollow

Fair Annie of Old Mule Hollow

by Beverly Courtney Crook

McGraw-Hill Book Company

New York St. Louis San Francisco Auckland Bogotá Düsseldorf Johannesburg London Madrid Mexico Montreal New Delhi Panama Paris São Paulo Singapore Sydney Tokyo Toronto

Library of Congress Cataloging in Publication Data

Crook, Beverly. Fair Annie of Old Mule Hollow.
SUMMARY: When Fair Annie, a sheltered mountain girl, inadvertently strays into forbidden McFarr territory her life opens up to tragedy and to love.
[1. Mountain life—Fiction] I. Title.
PZ7.C8816Fai [Fic] 78-9291
ISBN 0-07-014487-7

123456789 MUBP 78321098

For Judy, Steve, and Leslie

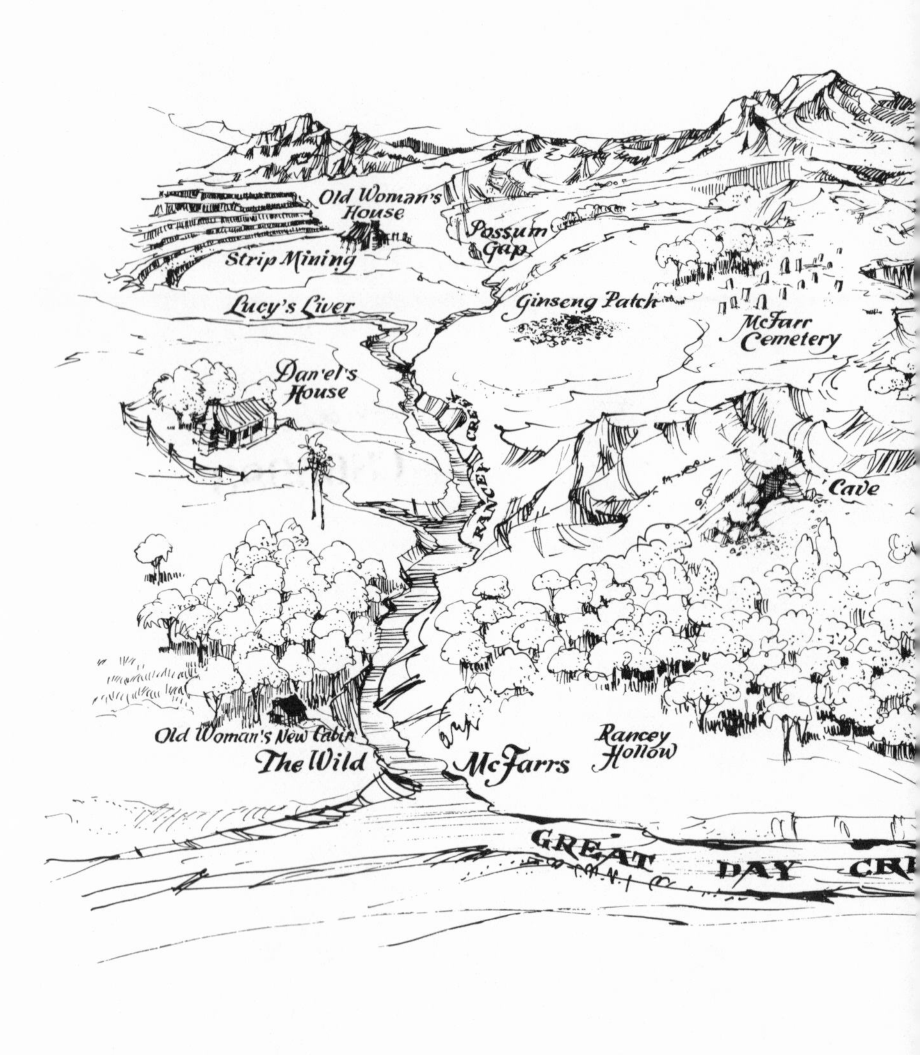
Old Woman's House
Strip Mining
Possum Gap
Lucy's Liver
Ginseng Patch
McFarr Cemetery
Dan'el's House
RANCEY CREEK
Cave
Old Woman's New Cabin
The Wild
McFarrs
Rancey Hollow
GREAT DAY

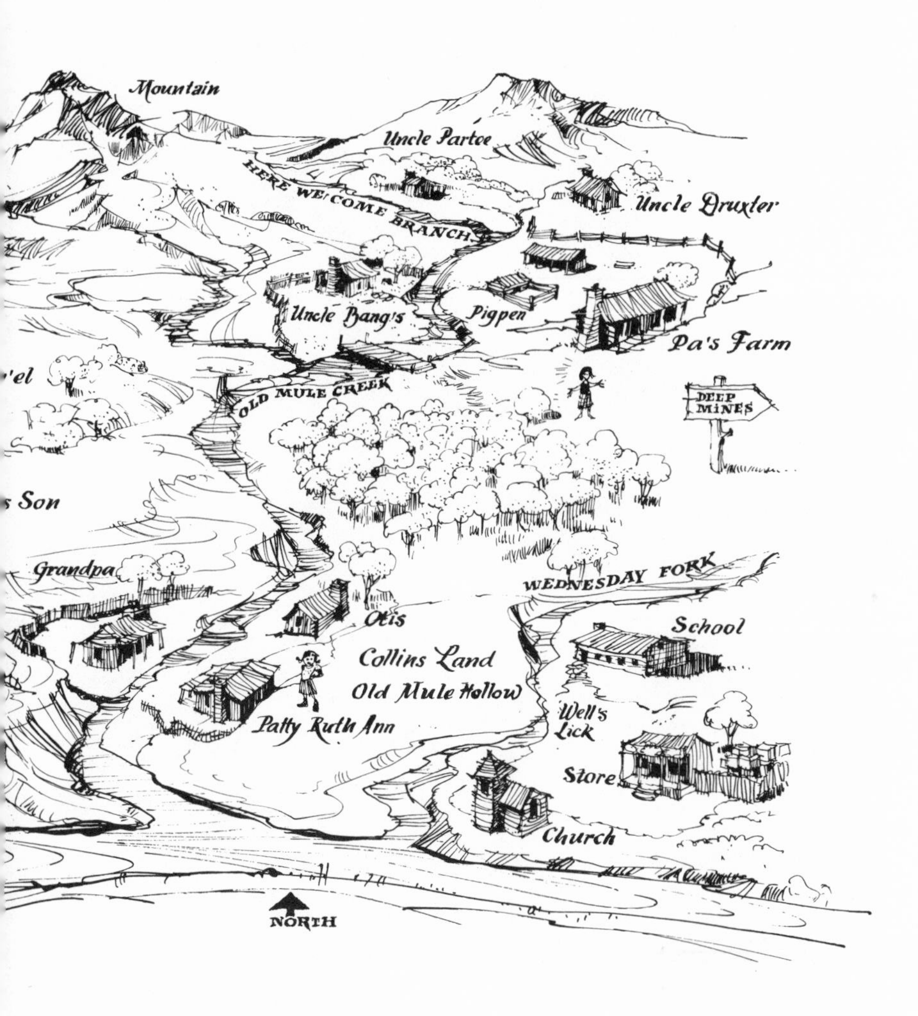

Mountain
Uncle Partoe
HERE WE COME BRANCH
Uncle Druxter
Uncle Bang's
Pigpen
Pa's Farm
OLD MULE CREEK
DEEP MINES
Grandpa
WEDNESDAY FORK
Otis
School
Collins Land
Old Mule Hollow
Well's Lick
Patty Ruth Ann
Store
Church
NORTH

Fair Annie of Old Mule Hollow

chapter one

A veil of mist drifted down from the mountaintops and settled on the unpainted cabins in Old Mule Hollow. Far up the valley, music mingled with the mist as someone plucked a haunting melody on a guitar.

Fair Annie Collins leaned against the rough boards of the pigpen and listened. That was *her* song—"Fair Annie of Roch Royal," the ballad that had inspired her name. She sang along softly:

> *"O who will shoe my bonny foot?*
> *And who will glove my hand?*
> *And who will kiss my rosy lips*
> *When you're in a foreign land?"*

Music was part of her life. Her whole family sang and played the old ballads and hymns that had been handed down for generations. The names of her brothers and sisters had come from songs, too: Barbara Allen, Mollie Vaughn, Nancy Belle, Lord Randal, and Sweet William. They were all proud of their names, except Sweet William. When he'd gone to school, which wasn't often, the kids had made fun of his name; so Pa had changed it to S. William Collins. Her brother liked that better. In fact, he liked it so well, he learned to write it.

The music, like everything else in Old Mule Hollow, was made by a Collins. Ever since Josiah Collins, a Scotsman, had been given this land on the West Virginia–Kentucky border in return for fighting the British in the Revolutionary War, it had been home to his descendants. And it was a poor idea for anyone whose name wasn't Collins to come into the hollow uninvited.

Fair Annie entered the pigpen to check on the sow and her litter. It was her job to see that they were fed and safe; a few black bears and "painters" still roamed the hills. When the piglets were bigger, a couple would be kept for food and the others traded. Pa was mighty good at trading. But the survival of all their livestock was critical; otherwise they'd be left with only two alternatives—starving or accepting welfare. And Fair Annie didn't doubt that Pa would choose starving. He was a proud man.

A loud whoop interrupted the music, and Blue's Son, their nondescript hound-dog, howled in reply. The hollerer was Uncle Druxter, giving his evening cry. His house was miles away, near the head of the hollow, but sounds echoed down the valley and sometimes it seemed as if he were next door. Every evening, and occasionally in the morning as well, he let out a long, distinctive yelp. Just because he felt like it. Uncle Partee hollered, also, and there were hollerers all through the mountains. But Uncle Druxter was the loudest and best.

Fair Annie hurried to finish her chores before dark. Night came early in this deep valley. By five o'clock the sun was leaving, even though it was June and the days were longer.

"Hey, Sis!"

She turned and saw S. William on the path below the pigpen, his red-blonde hair aglow in the farewell rays of the sun.

"Yore spendin' so much time with them pigs, yore beginnin' to look like 'em," he teased.

Fair Annie picked up a handful of gravel and playfully threw it down on him. "They're still prettier than any of your girlfriends! You could kiss one of my pigs and not know the difference."

Lord Randal, who was walking behind S. William, laughed and egged her on. "Give hit to him, Annie! He asked for hit."

Lord Randal was twenty, the oldest of the Collins children. He was neither as tall nor thin as S. William, who'd just turned nineteen, but he was far more quiet and mature than his easygoing brother.

As usual on Saturday night, both boys were on their way to see girlfriends in the hollow. The Collinses didn't encourage friendships with outsiders.

There was never any doubt where Lord Randal was going. He'd been courting Betty Lou for years. She was eighteen now, and only too willing to marry him, but her folks kept postponing the wedding. They were getting welfare money from the government—"drawin' welfare"—and couldn't get along without her share.

There was no way to predict where S. William was headed. He didn't concentrate on any one girl, but spread his affections over a wide area. He had more girlfriends than any boy in Old Mule, and none of the girls seemed to mind that he seldom took anything seriously, including them.

As her brothers continued on their way, Fair Annie wondered whether Otis, her cousin several times removed, would stop by as he usually did on Saturday nights. He wasn't really a boyfriend. Pa didn't allow her to keep company, although she was fifteen, the same age her ma had been when she married.

"Nary bug-brained boy's goin' to bust up yore schoolin'," Pa said. And Pa's word was law.

Fair Annie was the first member of her family to go beyond the sixth grade. She didn't attend school regularly, only when the weather was warm enough for her bare feet and thin sweater. But she'd managed to pick up enough "learnin'" when she was present to reach the eighth grade. The family was proud of her; not that they said much about it, especially Pa. In true mountain tradition, he never revealed his feelings in words or expression. But somewhere he'd picked up the word "scholar," and he used it freely when talking about Fair Annie.

Otis hadn't run afoul of Pa's ban on boyfriends because he never made a formal call. He "jes' happened by" to say hello and bring news of his family farther down the hollow. Then, as long as he was there, he'd ask Fair Annie to play dominoes with him. So far, Pa hadn't objected. Probably because he hadn't noticed how regularly Otis "jes' happened by." When he did, that would be the end of it, because Pa had a plan. And he didn't want anything to interfere with it.

"Somebody in this family's got to keep ahead of the govermint and all them papers they're a-wantin' you to sign," he always said. "Might sign the wrong ones if you cain't rightly read. And somebody's got to talk good, too. That lights a fire under them govermint people forever studyin' poor folks . . . snoopin' 'round astin' a lot of durn-fool questions."

So Fair Annie had been selected to keep the "govermint" at bay, not only by studying "book learnin'," but by speaking it as well. And Pa permitted no backsliding.

An indignant shriek came from the weathered cabin on the hillside, reminding Fair Annie that tomorrow was Sunday—church day. Nancy Belle was getting her neck scrubbed. Every third Sunday, Preacher Barclay held a service in the little church at Wells Lick. Her whole family attended, except maybe S. William, who usually developed a painful ailment every third Sunday. But tomorrow was also baptizing Sunday, a very special occasion.

"Fair Annieee! Git a bucket of water on yore way in," Ma called from the house.

She went obediently to the well, glad for an excuse to stay away a little longer. Since Patty Ruth Ann had been visiting them, things weren't quite the same.

The well was simply an open pipe sunk deeply into the ground, and drawing up water was a back-breaking job. She heaved and pulled with all the strength of her arms, until she'd finally lifted out the heavy bucket. Then she rested for a moment, watching the long shadows creep down the hillside where Pa and her brothers struggled to raise crops in the rocky soil.

Pa had once been a miner, working in the deep underground coal mines, just as his father, grandfather, and all the Collins men had done. The mountains were rich in coal, and no one could foresee a time when there wouldn't be jobs for miners. But that time came when machines were invented that could cut off a mountain and take the coal from the top. Then miners were no longer needed to dig underground, and Pa and the others lost their jobs. Some moved away and others accepted help from the government in the form of welfare checks.

But not Pa. He was one of the few still opposed to government handouts. "A man shouldn't ast the govermint to take care of him when he can take care of hisself," he told anyone who'd listen. "Govermint's goin' to bust down from all this takin'."

So instead of taking, Pa turned to farming, although

neither he nor the soil was especially suited for the job. But it provided food and, more important, independence.

"Annieee! I'm waitin'!"

Reluctantly she picked up the bucket. Her cousin Patty Ruth Ann was probably telling the family more about the wonderful things she'd seen and done in Baltimore. Whenever Fair Annie listened to these stories, a strange discontent swept over her. It was so disturbing, she wished her cousin hadn't come back.

Patty Ruth Ann had moved to the city last year and was living with her two older sisters, Bertha and Flossie. Now she wore nice clothes and shoes because they were all "drawin' welfare." But this visit back to the hollow had been unexpected. According to Patty Ruth Ann, one of the social worker ladies in the city had been coming home to Kentucky for a vacation and had offered her a ride so she could visit her folks. The only trouble was, her folks were scattered throughout the hollow right now. Their cabin near the mouth of Old Mule Creek had been flooded when heavy rains made the creek overflow, and they'd been living with other Collinses until it dried out. Patty Ruth Ann needed a place to stay, so Pa had decided they would make her welcome. After all, she was kin—although not exactly a favorite kin.

The more her cousin talked about life in the city, the more restless Fair Annie felt. Her world was bounded by the hills, where nothing ever happened; but Patty Ruth Ann had given her a glimpse of a different world—one filled with clothes, boyfriends, and excitement. She couldn't help feeling envious.

"Annieee!"

Staggering under the weight of the bucket, Fair Annie went back to the cabin. Barbara Allen and Billy were sitting in the handmade rocking chairs on the sagging front porch, while Mollie Vaughn and her Jimmy sat in the swing. She and Jimmy were going to get married as soon as he found a job, which wasn't likely to be soon, because he wouldn't leave the hollow. And there just weren't any jobs here now that the deep mines had closed. Jimmy had left once, back in 1963, but hadn't stayed away more than three weeks. By that time, he was so homesick for the hills, he had to come back. That had been two years ago and, although he kept promising to look for work outside again, here he was. And here he'd probably stay.

In the dwindling light, Fair Annie could see someone else on the porch . . . Otis! Laughing and talking with Patty Ruth Ann, who was all dressed up in her welfare dress and shoes. Fair Annie felt like dumping the bucket of water on Otis's head. Only she doubted that he'd look up; he was so busy staring at her cousin.

Fair Annie went around to the back door and entered the cabin. A large metal washtub occupied the center of the kitchen floor. Nancy Belle, the youngest of the family, was seated in it, bitterly complaining about the removal of a week's worth of dirt.

"My neck's all peeled like a turnip," she sobbed to Fair Annie. Nancy Belle was nine and at a stage where she seemed to be all arms and legs. When Ma pronounced her clean, she clambered out of the tub like a giant spider.

Ma added more water to the tub and Fair Annie decided to take her turn. She didn't trust herself to go back to the porch where Otis, who almost certainly had come to see *her*, was letting Patty Ruth Ann wrap him around her little finger.

Fair Annie wasn't in love with Otis, or anything. He was just the only boy who'd ever paid much attention to her. And besides, she hated to see him make a fool of himself over an older woman—Patty Ruth Ann was seventeen! S. William ought to tell Otis about the time he courted an older woman—almost twenty. Before he knew it, he was headed for the altar . . . came to his senses just in time. But it would serve Otis right if he got stuck with Patty Ruth Ann.

With nothing else to do after her bath, Fair Annie prepared for bed. Most evenings Pa took down his old banjo and Lord Randal tuned up his "dulcimore," and they sang before bedtime. But not on Saturdays because of all the visiting.

She went into the small bedroom that had been added onto the log cabin for the girls. A similar room had been added beside it for the boys, while the main part of the cabin served as a combination living room and bedroom for her parents. The only other room was the kitchen. The "bathroom" was an outhouse in the back yard.

Nancy Belle was already in the double bed that she shared with Fair Annie and Mollie Vaughn. And now that Patty Ruth Ann was here, the four of them had to squeeze into it. Barbara Allen was the only one with a bed of her own. At seventeen, she was the oldest girl and rated a narrow cot all to herself.

Fair Annie put on underclothes and added her old sweater over her slip as Nancy Belle wriggled into her special crevice in the center of the mattress. From long-ingrained habit, Fair Annie whispered her prayers before getting into bed. She wanted to pray that Patty Ruth Ann's welfare dress and shoes would fall apart, but she resisted the temptation. Instead, she prayed that this spell of discontent would pass. And if it wasn't asking too much, perhaps a pretty young man could be sent her way—someone more faithful than Otis.

The laughter and chatter on the porch grew louder, and Pa ended it by announcing that it was bedtime.

"If I'd knowed Cousin Otis was going to turn out so handsome, I might of stayed in the hollow," Patty Ruth Ann joked as she and Mollie Vaughn tried to find room in the crowded bed. Fair Annie clung to the edge to keep from falling out.

"Well, Jimmy's mighty pretty, too, but I'd better not catch you lookin' cross-eyed at him," Mollie Vaughn said. And she wasn't joking.

"Listen, the city's full of good-looking boys; I can have my pick of 'em," Patty Ruth Ann bragged. "And they have jobs, too . . . can buy you nice things." She paused, then asked, "You been thinking about what I said, Fair Annie? We'd be pleased to have you move in with us. You could ride back to Baltimore with me when Miz Davis comes for me. She's the social worker I told you about—the one that brought me. She wouldn't mind."

Before Fair Annie could reply, Mollie Vaughn grunted her disapproval. "Pa'll tan yore hide if you don't go back to school."

"But the schools in the city are better than the one here," Patty Ruth Ann protested. "I think Uncle Ned would let her go. You and Jimmy'd be smart to leave, too. He'd find a job there for sure."

"We'll manage," Mollie Vaughn said shortly. "Now let's git some sleep. Ma'll be roustin' us out early to git ready for church."

"Good night," Barbara Allen said from her cot. She was usually so quiet, it was easy to forget that she was around. But no one forgot Mollie Vaughn. Like S. William, she was lively and always close to laughter. But unlike her brother, she could be sharp-tongued with those she didn't like. And she definitely wasn't fond of Patty Ruth Ann.

Fair Annie lay awake thinking. She wasn't too fond of her cousin, either, and she suspected that there was more behind her invitation than she'd let on—probably another welfare check was the real motive. Patty Ruth Ann had said that she and her sisters didn't have to work because the government took care of them, so one more person living with them and receiving welfare would mean more money for all of them.

Still, it would be exciting to live in the city. And maybe she'd even find a pretty young man there. Anyway, what did she have to lose? There wasn't any future here. She was beginning to see that . . .

She fell asleep without making a decision.

chapter two

The ground was still cool beneath her bare feet when Fair Annie and the rest of her family trudged down the narrow, dirt mountain road on their way to church. They were strung out, single file, and stuck to the road, except when they had to detour around boulders that had sloughed off the mountainside and blocked the way. The stones hurt her feet, but she was used to that and never complained. None of her sisters had shoes, either.

Pa led the group and didn't allow a lot of noise, this being the Sabbath. Occasionally he glanced back to make sure that S. William was behind him. Whenever Pa told his son that it was time to go to church or answer to him, it produced a miraculous cure of S. William's third-Sunday ailment.

Lord Randal came next on the path; then Ma in her best cotton print; and Barbara Allen, her long blonde hair tumbling to her shoulders in soft waves. Fair Annie thought that, even in a patched dress, she was prettier than anybody. Especially prettier than Patty Ruth Ann, all gussied up today in a welfare dress with yards of ruffles. Fair Annie was glad to learn that after church her cousin was going to spend the day with her parents, who were staying with Aunt Nestor and Uncle Partee. At least she wouldn't be around if Otis came by again.

Dark-haired Mollie Vaughn was next in line. Tall and slim, she moved with an easy grace. But she was quieter than usual; probably thinking about Jimmy's lack of a job.

Fair Annie was supposed to be last on the road, to make sure that Nancy Belle didn't lag behind. But the small, wiry girl kept darting off at every opportunity. Fair Annie pushed her straight blonde hair behind her ears so that she could keep a closer watch on her sister's antics. Ma always defended Nancy Belle, but the older children considered her a natural-born pest.

Although the family members walked purposefully along and seemed to pay little attention to their surroundings, they were keenly aware of everything around them. Almost subconsciously, Fair Annie observed a woodpecker hammering a dead tree, a snake coiled on a rock, the pink of the laurel blooms, and the fresh green of the woods. These were things she'd known all her life and had taken for granted—until lately, when rumors of strip mining began to circulate. She didn't know much about stripping, only that it meant destruction of the land wherever it happened. Everyone said so.

Pa called over his shoulder, "Partee's boy heerd them miners is still over yonder in Stemmers Run, but the Bensons has quit fightin' 'em . . . jes' give up. You boys hear any give-out 'bout that?"

S. William replied, "Uncle Druxter says he talked to one of them Bensons down at the store. Said they're messin' up Stemmers almighty good; bulldozin' ever' livin' thing off'n the face of the earth. The Bensons have to move, but they don't know where they're a-goin'."

Lord Randal offered some additional information: "Tom Wells heerd some outsiders is tryin' to help . . . askin' the govermint to step in. Hit's the same people what sent that paper 'round to sign. Don't know what happened to that."

"Nothin' most likely," Pa said. "Hit don't do no good to ast the govermint to holp. We'll all be dead and buried 'fore they git hit writ down. Takes a ton of paper to do ary thing. If somethin' happened to paper, the govermint would be out of business."

"I saw them chopping off whole mountains when I was coming here with Miz Davis," Patty Ruth Ann chimed in. Pa hadn't asked for her comments, but he listened.

"They'd better not git any ideas about diggin' in this holler," he said threateningly. "I can still shoot a squirrel at three hundred paces."

The children nodded in agreement and felt reassured. Pa had a mighty sharp eye.

The day grew warm as the sun cleared the mountaintops and looked down into the valley. They'd had a long, dusty walk and were glad to see Wells Lick come into sight. Here between Great Day Creek and Wednesday Fork, the church, school, and store stood close together, making this the center of the world for all the hollows in the surrounding hills.

The door of the little white church was propped open when they arrived, and members of the congregation were waving fans of leaves and paper to relieve the stuffiness inside. Fair Annie and her brothers and sisters took their places on the choir benches; they accounted for almost half of the group. Then Otis came in and sat down beside her. When he smiled at her in his special way, she was ready to forgive him for last night and to think up excuses for his behavior: Patty Ruth Ann's city clothes and wily ways had been too much for him. It wasn't his fault.

While waiting for the preacher to arrive, the choir warmed up with "When We Get to Heaven." Fair Annie sang joyously as her discontent faded away. Everything was right with the world again; things were just the way they were supposed to be. The folks who'd been saved sat at the front of the church, and those who had yet to be "called" sat in the back. And outside, the usual bunch of husbands and boys who preferred religion from a distance hung around the grocery store or sat under a tree drinking soda pop. Nothing had changed. And neither had Otis.

From the corner of her eye, Fair Annie saw him turn to look, not at her, but at Patty Ruth Ann, who was sitting in the pew with her parents. She was trying to act coy as she batted her eyes at Otis, and he responded by grinning like a possum.

Fair Annie felt the bottom fall out of her day. At that moment there was a rustle of excitement across the church. Preacher Barclay strode up the aisle, and two strangers entered behind him, choosing seats near the door. No one stared at them, but an alertness swept over the congregation. She could feel the tension.

More often than not, outsiders brought trouble and were unwelcome. But Fair Annie felt sure that one of the strangers could do no wrong. He was the prettiest young man she'd ever seen. Otis looked homely in comparison. The older man with him had been here before, she remembered. He was a friend of the preacher. Some said he wrote down hymns because folks outside didn't sing them anymore.

Preacher Barclay had only one Sunday a month to get to work on sinners, and he wasted no time in preliminaries. "The Great Day of Judgment is coming!" he announced, getting right down to business. "Those who accept salvation will be with their loved ones in the heavenly choir, but sinners will spend eternity in the fires of hell. And that's the gospel truth!"

He lowered his voice. "The choice is yours, brothers and sisters." Then, with a dramatic burst that made her jump, he flung up his arms and shouted, "You can't have it both ways! You can't sin and be saved!"

The tempo of the sermon increased, and the congregation sat entranced. The preacher removed his coat, opened his collar, and mopped his face as he paced up and down exhorting sinners to repent. "Amens" from the congregation punctuated his statements, and before the sermon ended, two more members came forward to join the ranks of the saved.

Fair Annie tried to remember whether she'd done anything especially sinful recently. The preacher's description of hellfire was too vivid for comfort. But she couldn't concentrate on the sermon for long. In spite of the oral fireworks, her thoughts kept straying to the back of the church where the young stranger sat. What was he doing here? And where had he come from?

Immediately she tried to be practical to protect herself. Experience had taught her never to let her hopes get raised too high. The boy had come with the preacher and he'd leave with him, she told herself. She'd never see him again, so it didn't matter why he was here. The restlessness and discontent returned, only now it was worse than before. She'd never find a young man like that if she didn't leave these hills.

The sermon went on and on, ending finally with a brief prayer for Mr. Benson of Stemmers Run. Preacher Barclay, dripping with perspiration, sank into a chair and mopped himself dry while the choir and congregation sang the last hymn. Then everyone shook the preacher's hand, enthusiastically agreeing that he'd done some powerful preaching.

But there was more to come. Five people had been

waiting for warmer weather to be baptized, and this was the day. The congregation moved outside to the banks of Great Day Creek. The two strangers followed, and Fair Annie had a chance to study the younger man more closely. He was handsome, all right. And so were his clothes. Not at all like those sold in Mr. Wells's grocery store.

The water in the creek was down, as it always was in warm weather, so the preacher led his flock farther upstream to a deep pocket in Wednesday Fork. He waded to the middle of the fork, while Uncle Bangs and Tom Wells, the son of the store owner, stationed themselves between him and the bank to steady those coming out to be baptized. Pansy Collins was first. As soon as she entered the thick, dark water, the congregation, as if on signal, began singing, "Shall we gather at the river? The beautiful, the beautiful riverrr . . ."

The preacher held a handkerchief over Pansy's face and lowered her backwards until the rusty water covered her head. Then, sputtering and coughing, she was helped to the bank, her white dress stained an ugly red.

At the top of the mountains where the streams began, the waters were clear and sweet; but by the time they reached the mouth of the hollows, they ran red with iron washed out of unsealed and abandoned underground mines. Fortunately this stream, unlike some of the others, was free of acid that could eat into clothing and skin at a touch.

The baptizing continued, restrained at first, with just

the singing and the voice of the preacher heard above the running water. But soon emotions broke through mountain tradition and there was some weeping and shouting.

When it was over, the preacher, soggy to the waist, sloshed over to Pa and introduced the strangers. Fair Annie couldn't believe her eyes. Pa never had anything to do with outsiders if he could help it. The family edged closer, curious to find out what was happening. Fair Annie was so excited, she scarcely noticed that Otis was walking up the road with Patty Ruth Ann.

Reverend Barclay explained that his friend was writing down the old songs before they were forgotten. Fair Annie didn't understand how they could be forgotten when her kin sang them all the time.

"Outsiders don't sing much anymore," said the preacher, "and they don't teach their younguns to sing, either. The kids just listen to whatever's on their radios, and the old tunes are dying out. It's a sad thing."

The preacher's endorsement was good enough for Pa. Besides, he could size up a person better than most, and apparently he had decided that the men weren't here to make trouble.

"This here's Mr. Armour and his son Gene," Pa told his waiting family. "They come all the way from Burlsville to hear us sing, so I reckon we'll sing for 'em. They're comin' home with us." He introduced the family by rattling off their names until he came to Fair Annie. Then he added, as always, "She's a scholar!"

The Armours said they needed their "recorders" and

went back to the long, blue car parked in front of the store, where it had attracted a group of admirers. While he waited, Pa joined a knot of men discussing the latest strip mining rumors. Some had heard that stripping was about to start on Juniper Mountain. They all seemed relieved that it was McFarr land being threatened and not their own. But their jokes about the fate of miners who'd have to tangle with the wild McFarrs couldn't hide the worry that their land might be next.

The Armours returned with some black boxes and accompanied the family up the dirt road that was too rough to drive. Gene walked beside Fair Annie, and she felt a thrill of excitement just being near him. He was different from the boys in the hollow; even his language was different. He asked her about school, but before she'd worked up the courage to reply, her brothers started talking about cars and other dumb things. She just listened, taking in the boy's easy manner and handsome face. He was a sight to behold!

Mr. Armour admired the scenery. "I'm a mountain man, too," he told Pa. "Grew up in the mountains of Tennessee. I hate to think what strip mining might do to these beautiful ridges, but I understand they're working around here. The land's never the same afterwards, even though some of the coal companies boast about reclaiming it. Have you and your neighbors ever thought of going to court over stripping?"

"Well, I did put my mark on a paper back a-piece," Pa said. "Druxter's boy said hit might holp, but I have my doubts. Where there's money, there's power, and Devil take the hindmost. We jes' heerd they're a-goin' to strip 'round Juniper yonder . . . near McFarr land. Them McFarrs is ornery cusses, no doubt about hit, but for onct, I feel sorry for 'em."

The children realized that this was a big concession from Pa, because no Collins ever had a good word to say about a McFarr. There'd been bad blood between the clans for generations, although few remembered now how it had started. According to Great Aunt Eula, who got the story from her grandmother, the trouble began way back when game was still plentiful in the hills. The McFarr boys (there was practically an army of them then) would shoot at anything that moved; and they weren't too careful about staying on their own land. After they'd trespassed on Collins property once too often, Jake Collins decided to get even. He traded a mule for Tobias McFarr's cow, only he didn't mention that the mule was blind.

When Tobias found out, he didn't take the news kindly. He came into the hollow and shot every animal that Jake owned. Jake was so furious, he called in the law and had Tobias arrested, which set the whole McFarr clan on the warpath. They shot up the jail, wounded the sheriff, and released all the prisoners. Since then, tales of the "wild McFarrs" had grown with the years. And the deadly feud between the families waxed and waned, but never died.

As they neared the house, Ma and the girls hurried ahead to prepare dinner, while Pa stopped to show the strangers his hillside farm.

"T'ain't much," they heard him say, "but hit keeps body and soul together with nary a handout from the govermint. I'm still a free man, thank the Lord!" That freedom, according to Pa, was worth any sacrifice.

But Fair Annie was no longer sure. If Pa signed up for welfare, he'd get more money than he made farming. And she could buy clothes like Patty Ruth Ann's. Then maybe Gene would come back to visit her . . . sit on the front porch like her sisters' young men. . . .

Since early morning, dried string beans called "leather breeches," potatoes, and a chunk of salted pork fat had been cooking together on the iron stove, along with a big pot of coffee. Now, while Barbara Allen quickly made some large, round biscuits and put them in the oven, Mollie Vaughn opened a jar of "sass," canned last summer from the knotty apples on the ancient trees in the yard. Fair Annie and Nancy Belle arranged the plates on the table, making sure that the guests would get the ones with the fewest cracks. By the time the menfolk arrived, everything was ready.

"Dish hit up," Ma said, and they all sat down in the steaming kitchen. In accordance with mountain custom, Pa always took charge of any table conversation. None of the children spoke unless spoken to, and even Ma said no more than was necessary. But today Pa was content to listen. He was curious about this business of song collecting.

"I'm a lawyer by profession; I just collect songs as a hobby," the soft-spoken Mr. Armour told him. "When I discovered that the old songs were disappearing, I thought I'd better write them down before they were gone forever."

Then he went on to explain that the mountain ballads were mostly from the British Isles and centuries old, brought over to this country by the rugged men who first settled in the southern Appalachian highlands. Fair Annie was impressed. She'd no idea that her heritage went back so far, or that the songs she sang so casually were actually a legacy from the distant past.

She glanced shyly across the table at Gene. He wasn't looking at her, but she sensed that he'd been studying her. She self-consciously shoved a long strand of blonde hair out of her face and wiped the grease from her mouth with the back of her hand. If only she had on a welfare dress—one with lots of ruffles. Then maybe Gene would stare at her the way Otis looked at Patty Ruth Ann.

At the end of the meal Pa took down his banjo and Mr. Armour and Gene set up their recording machines. The family began to sing, starting with one of their favorites:

"On the top of yon mountain, where the green grass does grow;
Way down in yon valley, where the still waters flooow . . ."

When they'd finished, Mr. Armour adjusted his machine and let them hear themselves. It was beautiful! He played it again.

"Jes' like a band of angels!" Ma said softly.

Pa looked proud. He was ready to have them sing every song they knew. They sang more ballads, and Lord

Randal accompanied them on his handmade "dulcimore." Then they began on the hymns. They sang until their voices were hoarse and the Armours had used up their recording tape. Mr. Armour was quite pleased and kept thanking them for taking the trouble to oblige him.

"No trouble," Pa assured him. "We do a right smart of singin', even when nobody listens."

"I hope I can return the favor sometime," said Mr. Armour. "If you ever need any legal help, let me know. There's my address in Burlsville." He handed Pa a card.

When the Armours left, Pa sent all of the children to accompany them back to their car. This was insurance that no one in the hollow would mistake them for government men and hasten them on their way with a shotgun blast.

Just before driving off, Gene whispered, "Goodbye, Fair Annie. You really are fair!"

Then they were gone and she knew she'd never see him again. He didn't belong in the hollow; anybody could tell that.

As they walked back home, Fair Annie made a decision: She was going to leave. When Patty Ruth Ann returned to Baltimore, she'd go with her. There was nothing to hold her here—no job, no money, no young man like Gene. Only possum-faced Otis. And he'd never once told her that she was "fair." She didn't like the idea of living with her cousin, but if that was the only way to city life, she'd just have to take it.

A high-pitched yelp bounced along the ridge and

echoed through the valley. Uncle Druxter was giving his evening holler. Fair Annie wondered whether there were hollerers in Baltimore. Perhaps they yelled from the tops of tall buildings. Her thoughts were so full of Gene and going to the city, there wasn't room for pigs. For the first time, she neglected her nightly check on the sow and her litter.

chapter three

When Fair Annie paid her regular early morning visit to the pigpen, she was still wrapped in a fog of dreams about the new life she'd lead in the city. But she was quickly wrenched back to the realities of the hollow when she saw the wire covering on top of the pen. It was badly mangled, and the ground in front of the enclosure was stained by something red that looked like blood. Cold fear settled in the pit of her stomach. If the pigs were gone . . . She couldn't bring herself to think of the consequences.

She noticed now that Blue's Son wasn't around, trailing at her heels as he usually did. He was a good watchdog and could frighten or bluff most any crittur. So why hadn't he driven off whatever had been here? Unless . . . unless it had been a bear; he'd be no match for that. Yet she didn't doubt that he'd do his best.

She took a deep breath to steel herself against what she was certain she'd find in the rough shelter that housed the pigs. She peered in. Amazing! The sow and her piglets were still there, cowering in a corner and trembling with fright. She counted them. One was missing!

Fair Annie examined the wire over the pen. Nothing very large could have entered through the torn place, she decided. But only something large could have twisted it like that. The evidence was pointing more and more strongly to a bear, although none had been around for years. Hunting had all but cleaned them out of the hollow.

Glancing down, she noticed that a board at the bottom of the shelter was loose. A small pig could have pushed out there and not have been able to get back in. She picked up a rock and hammered the nails in tightly, then worked the wire into place over the pen. Lord Randal and S. William would have to hunt out this new enemy before it did more damage. But she dreaded telling them about the missing pig. Or dog!

She stooped to touch the spots near the pen, and her fingertips turned red—blood! Something had been injured or killed here. She didn't want to believe that it was Blue's Son. She loved that floppy-eared old dog. The family had once had a dozen dogs, including Blue Boy, the best hunting dog around. But as Pa found it harder to make ends meet, he'd gotten rid of them all, except Blue and one of his puppies. Eventually Blue Boy died, and now Blue's Son was the only dog left. He was supposed to belong to her brothers, but he'd adopted her and was a constant companion.

Fair Annie whistled a high, pulsating call that always brought the dog at a run. This time he didn't come and she heard no bark or whimper. She could see drops of blood leading away from the pen toward the slope, and she began following them. The dog might be injured . . . or dying, she thought. Losing a pig was bad enough, but Blue's Son was just like a member of the family.

The trail of blood led down the hillside, all the way to Old Mule Creek. Even there she saw a red spot on a stone and bloody signs up the opposite slope, so she crossed the creek on the fragile swinging bridge that spanned it.

As she drew dangerously close to the end of Collins land and the beginning of McFarr territory, she found herself thinking up excuses to abandon the search. The blood might have come from an injured raccoon . . . or possum . . . or from the pig when something carried it off. The dog was probably enjoying a good nap somewhere. But she knew deep down that whatever'd bothered the pigs had not gone unchallenged by Blue's Son.

She was getting farther and farther away from familiar landmarks and feeling more and more uneasy. Although the McFarrs had withdrawn into their hollow and were seldom seen anymore, the tales about them lived on. In fact, the air of mystery that now surrounded them made them seem more fearsome than ever. No one could be sure what they were up to, but the Collinses were convinced that it was nothing good.

At the top of the ridge she could actually see into Rancey Hollow—a place where no one except McFarrs dared set foot. Then she saw more signs of blood and crept cautiously down the slope, right into the forbidden land.

She followed the spots to the base of a huge rock, where there was a large smear. But there the trail ended. Using a stick, she shuffled the dead leaves on the ground and poked around a thick stand of azaleas that not long ago had set the mountains ablaze with their orange-red flowers. But the red of blood was missing; there were no further clues.

In the midst of her search, something made her look up. Standing silently above her on the rock was a tall, loose-jointed boy with a rifle resting on his shoulder. His faded overalls and shirt were even more ragged than her own clothes, and his shaggy, dark hair looked as if it had been hacked off with a knife. The most startling thing about him were the straight, black brows over piercing blue eyes. They gave him a menacing appearance, like a hawk about to swoop down on its prey. He was an awesome sight. And, she suddenly realized, it was one that she'd never hoped to see—a wild McFarr at close range!

They stared at each other for several minutes as she considered whether it would be better to be shot running away or to stay and be shot on the spot.

With an effortless motion, the boy lowered the rifle

from his shoulder and cradled it in his arm. "You going to stand there all day with your mouth open?" he asked.

She gulped. "I was looking for Blue's Son . . . a dog . . ."

"A liver-colored crittur?"

She nodded.

"He tangled with a bear." He pointed to the bloody smear nearby. "Old Brutus, I call him. He's raided our barn twice. Must be too old to hunt anymore. But once a bear gets a taste for livestock, there's no stopping him. I hated to shoot him, but it had to be done."

"But what about Blue's Son?"

"A good dog! He'd been hurt, but stuck right on that bear's heels. Seemed to be after a pig Brutus was carrying off. I saw 'em and tried to take aim, but it was getting dark and your dog kept getting in the way. I finally got a clear shot, but not before Brutus took a swipe at the dog. Lucky for him he didn't get the full force of the blow or he'd be dead. I'll take you to him."

Fair Annie though this must be a dream. Or a nightmare! She couldn't possibly be standing here listening to a wild McFarr. But he didn't seem dangerous. In fact, he spoke rather politely, like Gene. And his speech had more shadings of the outside than of the mountains.

"Are you . . . you are a McFarr, aren't you?"

"I am, for true. And I reckon you're a Collins."

"Yes, Fair Annie."

"Well, Fair Annie. I'm Dan'el. Come on, if you want to see your dog."

He started up the mountain, moving swiftly with the economy of motion characteristic of mountain men. He seemed as much at home on these wooded hills as the squirrels and deer.

"I carried him up here to a certain place I know. He was bleeding bad and I thought he ought to stay quiet."

Fair Annie followed meekly, never doubting that he was telling her the truth, but frightened all the same.

He waited for her to struggle up the slope that he had walked up with no more effort than if it had been level. But then he wasn't barefoot, and she was. She could see him standing up there, tall and proud, the sharp eyes taking in every detail of the woods. She didn't think that he was much older than she was—sixteen or seventeen, perhaps; yet she felt dwarfed by his presence, as if one of the mighty oak trees had come to life and was leading her around. After all, a McFarr wasn't something you saw every day. They'd always seemed as foreign as China or Timbuktu.

The boy didn't say anything else, and he didn't seem to expect her to speak, which didn't surprise her. That was the way of mountain men. He just led her farther into the woods along a twisting route, until they came to a large outcropping of rock. Then he announced, "He's here."

She didn't see the dog anywhere and suspicion flared. What better place to get rid of a Collins! No one would find her for years.

The boy said, rather defensively, "I didn't know whose dog he was. I just cared for him as best I could, because I can't stand to see an animal suffer. But he's not ready to walk yet. He's lost a lot of blood."

He turned, looking directly at her with those frightening eyes, and said, "I'd take it kindly if you'd forget about this place once you leave. Strangers coming around here could get themselves killed."

"I understand."

He smiled unexpectedly and led her around the outcropping. There she saw two large boulders standing on end like the portals of a gate. He suddenly vanished between them, and it wasn't until she got closer and viewed it from the proper angle that she could see the opening.

As she entered, he struck a match, revealing a dome-roofed cave, about as big as the main part of their cabin. When he used the match to light a candle in a holder fastened to the rock wall, she saw Blue's Son lying on a bed of straw. He had strips of torn cotton cloth wound around his ribs, and he whimpered as she approached. He even managed to wag his tail slightly but was too weak to stand.

Dan'el pulled back an edge of the bandage for a critical look. "I was afraid of that. Wound's infected. Bear claws usually make a fester. My uncle got swiped by a bear once. Made an unholy amount of pus."

"What did you do for it? Maybe we could do the same thing for Blue's Son."

"Old Woman fixed him up. She's the only one around who can do that—cures better than any doctor. I was on my way to Possum Gap to see her when I spotted you. I'm afraid your dog's not going to make it without some right good help."

Fair Annie hadn't realized until now just how badly injured the dog was. She wanted to cry, but held back the tears. She'd never forgive herself if she broke down in front of this boy. As a matter of pride, she had to show him that the Collinses weren't weaklings.

"Do you think she'd help me?" she asked, speaking with difficulty because of the lump in her throat. She'd heard about Old Woman's miraculous cures. The tales had spread to Old Mule Hollow years ago, but she'd thought they were largely myth, like the other stories that were repeated and embroidered so often that they eventually bore little resemblance to the original.

"She'll help you if I ask her," Dan'el replied confidently. "But we ought to take her something. It's only polite."

Fair Annie spread her hands. "I haven't anything with me." She didn't have anything worth giving at home, either, but she didn't mention that.

"I know just the thing," Dan'el said as he started up the mountain with his easy, rhythmic gait.

She tried to imitate his stride but found it impossible. It was something boys were born with, she decided. S. William moved like that. He could range through the hills all day without getting tired. But she didn't know of any girls who could do it.

They were following a barely perceptible path—a "trace" that the Indians had used long before the McFarrs or Collinses pushed them from these hills.

Suddenly Dan'el paused and took his bearings. "Over

this way." Leaving the path and turning to the right, he entered a partially shaded cove of poplar and beech. In the distance was a clearing where white tombstones dotted the hillside.

"Here it is!" he cried.

He was standing in a patch of green-leaved plants, some of them several feet tall. Fair Annie looked closely at a large plant. The top of its main stem had branched into several smaller ones, each with three big leaves and two little ones.

"Why, it's sang! My uncles are always looking for it, but it's hard to find in Old Mule anymore."

"Dealers buy it up. Pay big money for the roots, so people get greedy about it. They dig it too young and don't put back the seeds to start new plants."

"Ma says it'll cure rheumatism."

"Old Woman uses it for lots of ailments, especially 'the allovers.' That's what she calls nervousness. Her grandfather was a seaman, she told me, and sailed around the world. He found out that the Chinese have used sang for hundreds of years. It's real name is 'ginseng.' "

"Is this what you're going to take to Old Woman?"

Dan'el nodded. "But only because she's completely out. It shouldn't be dug this early—not before August."

He picked up a stick and carefully pushed the soil from around a plant. In a few minutes he lifted out a long, slender root resembling a human figure, the two-pronged end being the legs.

He stopped suddenly to look down the wooded slope,

as if something had caught his eye. Fair Annie followed his gaze. There below them on the slope was one of the tallest, gauntest men she'd ever seen, staring in their direction. He didn't speak or change expression and, in a matter of seconds, vanished into the forest.

She was certain that he'd gone to warn the other McFarrs about the stranger on their land.

chapter four

"Who was that?" Fair Annie asked Dan'el as he tucked the ginseng root into his pocket.

"Pap. Out for a little hunting."

"Will you get a lickin' for talkin' to a Collins? I'd hate to bring you to grief."

"I don't get lickin's," he stated matter-of-factly. "My pappy knows I wouldn't be doing anything to bring harm to my generations. Besides, there's not much going on around here that he doesn't know about. He probably knows about your dog without anybody telling him."

Fair Annie wasn't convinced that the McFarrs would

accept her presence so readily. As soon as she doctored poor old Blue's Son, she planned to hightail it out of here and never come back. She had "the allovers" bad.

They had been climbing steadily, and she thought they must have reached the highest point on this wooded ridge. Instead, she discovered that the mountaintop seemed to be folded over, and they were in a tiny, protected valley beneath the overhanging peak. Nestled into this pocket was a clearing watered by a small stream; and back against the mountain, she saw a lone, weather-beaten shack. It looked uninhabited except for the split-bottom rocker on the tilted porch.

"This is Possum Gap," Dan'el said. "Hope Old Woman's home. She doesn't go far anymore, but she still collects herbs around here for her medicines. I reckon city doctors could learn a lot from her."

As they approached the shack, dogs in assorted shapes, sizes, and colors raced out of nowhere and raised the alarm. Fair Annie was afraid they might do more than bark if she went any closer.

"They're just announcing us," said the boy, striding forward. Fair Annie kept close behind him as he knocked on the door.

Immediately it was opened by a small, white-haired woman, whose lined and shriveled face resembled a dried-out potato. She squinted at her visitors and smiled.

"Come in, children. I been expectin' you. I can always tell when visitors are on the way. Mighty glad to see you, Dan'el." She studied Fair Annie for a moment, then exclaimed, "Why, you're a Collins! Ain't seen nary of your kin for quite a spell—maybe fifty years. And that's the truth."

She invited them into the log cabin, which was neat and clean but on the verge of collapse. Holes between the logs had been plugged with newspapers and cans to keep out the wind, and the room smelled of dampness.

Dan'el held out the ginseng root they had dug, and sheer delight crept across the woman's face. "I didn't think I was ever goin' to git ary bit of sang agin. Cain't walk that fur now. I'm mighty obliged to you, younguns." She looked at them questioningly. "You need somethin'? Magic, or medicine?"

"We need some medicine for Fair Annie's dog. He's been mauled by a bear, and the wound's infected."

"That don't sound good," said the woman sympathetically, "but I'll fetch you my special sab. Used hit on myself awhile back when a scratch got festered. Cleared hit up jest as pretty!"

While she talked, she rummaged in an old orange crate that served as a cabinet. It was set on end and curtained by a piece of cloth nailed across the front. The woman removed several jars and bottles, and after mixing their contents, seemed satisfied that she'd concocted the right remedy. As a final step, she used a twig broom to brush down some cobwebs from the rafters and added them to the mixture—"to stop the bleedin'."

"There! That ought to do hit!" Old Woman announced so confidently that Fair Annie was ready to believe it really would work. "Now go git it on the crittur as soon as you can. The longer you wait, the worse hit'll be. But come back when you can set a spell."

She saw them to the door and yelled at the barking dogs to be quiet. "They's friends," she told the pack, and they subsided. "You come back now and visit Old Woman agin," she called after them a little wistfully.

"We will," Dan'el promised, but Fair Annie was sure she'd never set foot on this land again.

She raced behind Dan'el as he moved rapidly down the mountain. In a moment he took off in a new direction. When she finally caught up with him, they were in a densely wooded grove where another stream had cut out a valley that looked very much like the one where she lived. Only this one was wilder, more undisturbed, and so shaded by beech and oak trees that it was in perpetual twilight.

In a remote corner of the valley stood a log cabin, completely isolated and almost invisible. It was not unlike the usual mountain cabin, except it appeared more sturdy and not at all run-down.

Dan'el said, "We'll need fresh bandages. Do you have anything you could tear?" After a glance at her clothes, he added, "I reckon not. I'll see what we have."

When he went up on the front porch, she hung back. Going through the woods was one thing, but barging in on his folks was something else. She'd heard about the terrible McFarrs all of her life; and although this boy had been friendly so far, she couldn't count on the whole family reacting the same way.

"It's all right," he told her. "Anyway, nobody's home."

"How about your ma?"

"She's dead. Nobody lives here now but me and Pappy."

"Where're your brothers and sisters?"

"Haven't got any. Now come on and help me tear some cloth, unless you want that dog of yours to get worse."

That moved her, and she followed him timidly into the house. "You mean you don't have any brothers and sisters at all?" This seemed incredible. She didn't know anyone who was an only child.

"Nope. Mama died a couple of years ago, so Pap and I fend for ourselves."

Fair Annie stopped just inside the door and stared in amazement. She'd never been in a cabin like this in all her life. Two whole walls were covered with shelves. But the shelves weren't filled with jars of canned food, shecky beans, or dried pumpkin—the only purpose for shelves at home. These held books—dozens of them—from floor to ceiling. There weren't that many books at the school at Wells Lick.

Dan'el sorted through some worn shirts and selected the worst one, although it actually wasn't any more rotten than the one he had on.

"This'll do," he said, and ripped off some strips. "Now you roll while I tear," he ordered.

Fair Annie obeyed, but she couldn't keep her eyes off the books. "Who reads all those books?" she asked finally.

"I do. Most of them belonged to my mother. She used to be a schoolteacher before she married my father."

He had gathered up the torn strips and left the cabin, walking so fast she had trouble hearing what he was saying. And she didn't want to miss any of it. No one knew much about the McFarrs, except that they were wild and likely to blow your head off if you trespassed. They were rarely seen—only when one or two of them dropped by Wells's grocery for food or mail. That was all. Now she was curious to find out more, yet afraid to pry.

"You've read *all* those books?"

"Yep. Mama used to teach me from them. She taught Pap, too, although he didn't take to it so much. He was always too busy keeping us fed. She said that she could give me a better education than I'd get at Wells Lick, so she taught me all the time. Thought I might go to the university someday."

The boy seemed eager to talk, as if making up for lost time, so she risked another question.

"Your ma born around here?"

"No, in South Carolina. My grandpappy has a textile mill there. He's right well off. Mama met Pap when he was a soldier during World War Two, helping to fight Hitler. Her kin said she wasn't going to marry any hillbilly—even got the sheriff after Pap for something he didn't do. So they ran away and got married and came back here to Rancey Hollow, where the McFarrs have always lived. Nobody bothered them after that. Couldn't find 'em, I reckon. It's pretty rugged in here."

"Haven't you ever met your grandparents?"

"Yeah. Mama and her folks eventually buried the hatchet. She took me to visit them a couple of times, and they started sending books . . . still do. So Pappy just keeps building more shelves."

If the boy hadn't been along, Fair Annie would have walked right by the cave. It was difficult to find because this patch of rocks looked very much like the other rocky areas on the mountainside.

Blue's Son was sick, she could tell that right off. Fair Annie wondered whether he was going to live. This medicine would have to be mighty strong to save him.

"Old Woman's a good doctor," Dan'el reassured her. "She used to be a granny woman, too. Took care of Mama when I was born. She's getting too old for that anymore, but she can still cure a lot of sickness. We're lucky she had this stuff on hand."

Fair Annie wished she shared his faith in the awful-smelling,sticky ointment that he was applying to the dog's ripped side. Then he deftly wrapped the strips of torn shirt over the wound and brought a tin can of water close enough for the dog to drink.

She looked around the cave. It had been used for more than a dog shelter, she thought. A bale of straw appeared to have been made into a bed, and the candle and other items indicated that the boy might have slept here occasionally. It didn't look uncomfortable, but rather cozy with the candle burning.

"You won't be able to move him now," Dan'el said. "He's too heavy for you to carry, and he can't walk."

"But who'll take care of him? I can't come back again. Pa'd skin me if he knew I'd crossed over here."

The boy looked at her with those piercing eyes that seemed to see right through her, and she was reminded once again that she was dealing with a dangerous breed—something she tended to forget with Dan'el. He was very gentle for a McFarr.

"I'll look after him," he said quietly. "You can come see him when you want. No one will bother you. But . . ." He hesitated. "He's too sick to eat right now, but he should have something later."

She understood what he was trying to say: He'd look after the dog, but feeding him was another matter. Obviously his kin weren't drawing welfare and didn't have extra food.

"I'll bring something, but I'm not sure I can find this cave again."

"Come back after dinner and go to the place where you met me this morning. Whistle when you get there."

Against her better judgment, she gave silent consent. Dan'el then accompanied her to the top of the ridge that separated Rancey Hollow from Old Mule, and there he stopped. He pointed out the best route back down the slope, and she left, afraid to look back until she was safely on Collins soil. When she did turn, she caught a glimpse of him among the trees—an odd, shaggy-haired figure that quickly disappeared. But she was sure those keen eyes could follow her as precisely as any hawk. What a strange boy! Imagine reading all those books. But he'd saved Blue's Son, and she was indebted to him for that.

Fair Annie struggled up the hill to the pigpen. The pigs

were no longer frightened, just hungry. She'd gone off without feeding them. She didn't know how she was going to break the news that one was missing without also telling about Blue's Son. She'd have to give that some thought.

As she went toward the house, still sorting through the events of the morning, she bumped into Patty Ruth Ann, who was returning from visiting her folks. Fair Annie realized with alarm that her cousin must have been coming up the mountain road at the same time she was coming down the mountain from Rancey Hollow. If Patty Ruth Ann had seen her, she wouldn't waste any time in letting her know.

"I thought I was seeing things . . . you going so close to McFarr land. You trying to get yourself killed?" A sly smile crept over her cousin's face, and Fair Annie prepared for the worst.

"I wonder what your pa would do if he found out?"

"I was following some tracks. Something's been bothering the sow," she explained lamely, then felt ashamed for making excuses to the likes of Patty Ruth Ann. This was none of her business.

"Well, you can count on me not to tell. It won't make no difference, anyhow, if you're in Baltimore. But if you stick around here, maybe someone ought to let your pa know . . . just in case the McFarrs saw you and try to settle the score."

In spite of this threat, Fair Annie felt relieved. At least Patty Ruth Ann didn't know that she'd actually been on

McFarr land. And she hadn't seen Dan'el. He'd be even harder to explain.

As Fair Annie walked beside her cousin to the cabin, she studied the tall, large-boned girl who didn't resemble any of the rest of her kin, not even Flossie and Bertha, her sisters. Their mother'd been a Brown, she remembered, and the Browns were a peculiar lot—very talky. Patty Ruth Ann was just like them. She wondered whether Old Woman had a medicine that would permanently pucker a big mouth.

chapter five

Fair Annie hoped that no one would ask about her long absence. She was glad that Patty Ruth Ann didn't know that she'd been gone all morning, or she might tell about that, too. Normally the members of the family came and went without question, unless they failed to do their chores. But if her parents did ask where she'd been, Fair Annie would have no choice but to tell them. It had been instilled in her since birth that a lie was unworthy of a Collins.

As Pa put it, "The creek might run dry, the roof leak, and our luck plumb give out, but we always got one thing left, and that's our good name. We don't lie, and we don't cheat. And I reckon that's worth more'n gold any day in the week."

But Fair Annie needn't have worried. Much bigger problems were at hand when she entered the cabin. And no one would have listened if Patty Ruth Ann had decided to tattle.

"They're movin' in, Pa. Awful close," S. William was saying. "Tom Wells says they've got the biggest machines he ever seed. Big as a mountain!" The laughter had gone from his eyes, and he was deadly serious. "Some fellers at the store said hit's certain now. They're aimin' to strip mine that seam of coal on Juniper Mountain, up above Lucy's Liver. And you know that seam comes right acrosst Buckeye Mountain to the head of this here holler."

Pa sat rubbing the stubble on his chin, which indicated that he was giving the matter deep thought. Lord Randal sat by quietly, as they waited for Pa's pronouncement.

Finally it came: "I reckon we'd best not neglect our own field to plant our neighbor's. If them miners git this fur, we'll head 'em off. But I don't see there's much we can do til then. Them wild McFarrs always take care of theirselves, and they sure in thunder don't welcome nobody meddlin' in their business. So I say, we'd be fools to stick our noses in." He paused and rubbed a few more strokes before adding, with a sidelong glance at the boys, "Course if you come acrosst any way of stoppin' 'em . . ."

He left an opening for them to use their initiative without directly disobeying him. That was all they wanted. They looked more hopeful as they went to the back porch to wash up.

Patty Ruth Ann had been silent for about as long as was possible for her. Now she said, to no one in particular, "The McFarrs don't scare some folks."

Fair Annie held her breath and hoped that Pa wasn't paying attention.

"What're you talkin' about?" Ma asked her.

"Oh, jest that the McFarrs don't seem to watch their land like they used to."

Fair Annie wondered how far she'd go. She understood that this was just her cousin's way of getting what she wanted—in this case, making sure that Fair Annie went to Baltimore—but that was no excuse for . . . Patty Ruth Ann lost her audience as Barbara Allen sniffed and began to cry.

"I can't hold it in no longer. Billy's been drafted and has to join the Army. He won't be back for years!" The tears flowed faster.

Fair Annie put her arm around her sister's shoulder in a rare display of affection. The closely knit family shared emotions, along with everything else, but seldom demonstrated them.

"He'll come home on leave, jest like Uncle Bangs's boy," Mollie Vaughn said consolingly, while Pa fled to the porch. He couldn't stand tears, a sign of weakness and an embarrassment.

Fair Annie was sad for her sister but, at the same time, thankful that she'd diverted attention from Patty Ruth

Ann, who never knew when to stop once she started talking. Fair Annie had intended to tell her that she was willing to try city life and bring in another welfare check to help pay expenses, but now she'd let her wait to find out. Only there was a risk in waiting; it was hard to predict what Patty Ruth Ann might do next.

Barbara Allen's tears subsided, and Ma announced dinner. "Hit's ready, I reckon."

They sat down to their noon meal of beans cooked with the inevitable sow belly, biscuits, and molasses. And, of course, coffee. Since Pa was preoccupied, there was no conversation.

At the end of the meal, he casually said, "I have a mite of tradin' to do with Druxter," and set off for Here We Come Branch. But they all knew that while trading would be done, that wasn't his main goal today. He was worried about the mining and wanted a report from higher up in the hollow.

As Fair Annie helped clear away the dishes, she managed to stick a bit of leftover sow belly into the middle of a large biscuit and slip it into her pocket, watching all the while to be sure Patty Ruth Ann hadn't observed her.

Scraps for the dog were collected in an old baking tin kept in a corner of the kitchen, right beside the bucket of slop for the pigs. Ma added a little grease, but Fair Annie couldn't possibly carry the greasy mixture with her. While her mother and the girls were busy consoling Barbara Allen, she poured the food for Blue's Son into the pigs' bucket.

As soon as she could get away, Fair Annie went to the pigpen. She was supposed to clean it today, but that would have to wait. She stood poised on the hillside below the pen, glancing in all directions. When she was certain the coast was clear, she started down to Old Mule Creek, just as she'd done that morning. After crossing the swaying bridge, she went up the opposite slope as quickly as her bare feet would permit, stopping only to remove an occasional bur or nut shell from between her toes, or to wipe away blood from another stone cut.

Fair Annie wasn't accustomed to disobeying, and it made her uncomfortable to be doing it now. She hadn't actually been told not to go into Rancey Hollow; it was something that was understood. No Collins ever went on McFarr land, and woe to the McFarr who trespassed on Collins property. If she'd told Pa about Blue's Son, that wouldn't have changed things one bit. McFarr land was off limits, even if it meant the loss of the dog.

At last she reached the large rock where the smear of blood still remained on the leaves below it. Dan'el had told her to whistle, but she didn't want to attract any other McFarrs. She wet her lips and gave a soft, high trill that blended in with the woodland music of birds and insects.

Then she waited. There was no movement or sound to announce the boy's arrival. But suddenly there he was, standing on the rock and looking down at her just as before.

"I got something for Blue's Son," she said, holding out the biscuit that she'd wrapped in a broad mayapple leaf.

He simply turned and led the way to the cave, while she followed. As soon as she entered the cave, Blue's Son whimpered. Dan'el lit the candle on the wall, and she petted the dog to quiet him. When she offered the biscuit and meat, he showed little interest, but nibbled at it as if to please her. Then he tried to get up. Almost immediately a red spot appeared on the cotton bandage and began to spread.

"You'd better wait outside so he doesn't get excited," Dan'el said. "The bleeding's started again, but I think he's a little stronger, even though the medicine hasn't had much time to work."

She left, reluctantly, as the boy settled the dog back on its bed of straw and adjusted the bandage. She walked with the wind so Blue's Son wouldn't get her scent, and stood looking out over the foreign valley. She found it hard to believe that she was here, much less meeting a McFarr. And one was enough; she hoped she didn't meet up with any more of them.

This hollow was different from Old Mule, she noted. Here the slopes were rougher, the woods more dense, so that it stayed dark and gloomy; but enough sunlight penetrated in places to make the azaleas feel at home. Not far away, she could see a laurel slick—a treeless area where laurel, rhododendron, and blueberries grew in profusion over the rocks. Laurel in bloom was purely beautiful, she thought.

When she turned, Dan'el was standing beside her. "No better place than the mountains," he said. "Nice and quiet. And room to spread out. When Mama took me to Charleston to visit my grandparents, I felt like I couldn't breathe with all those people squeezed together. Not like this. Everything's pretty in these hills—even stinkin' benjamin." He pointed to a patch of little white flowers with pointed petals that she hadn't noticed.

"And look at that toadshade. See, it's all in threes." He showed her its three yellow flower petals and three green leaves. This flower was common in her hollow, but she hadn't really looked at it before.

"You know a lot about plants," she said.

"My mother knew them all by name. She liked to grow flowers, but they never did much around the cabin. Too shady, I reckon. So she had to be content with wildflowers. She'd take long walks just to see the different kinds. And I'd go with her. I remember she used to say that it wasn't enough to feed your body; you had to feed your soul, too."

Fair Annie thought that over. It was a queer way of talking, but she understood what it meant.

"Your hollow sure is thickety," she told him. "Beats Old Mule for rough going."

The boy gave one of his rare smiles. It began slowly and took a long time in coming. "It's thickety, all right, and that's what saved it from being logged years ago. My Grandpap McFarr told me about all the sawing and log runs in these hills. He'd heard about it from his grandpappy, because it started right after the War between the States, during the big building boom. Mountain folks needed money, so they let the loggers come in and cut the trees—thousands of them, beginning with the biggest and the best. Some of 'em had been here before Columbus. They cut everything . . . didn't leave seedlings to hold the soil, and it washed away. Nothing would grow. After that the railroads came in and coal mining got going, so they cut more timber to support the mine tunnels. If it hadn't been more trouble than it was worth to get in and out of Rancey Hollow, I reckon it'd been logged, too."

Fair Annie was awed by his knowledge. Not even her teachers at Wells Lick had told her this much history about her mountain home.

"Now it looks like stripping's going to do more damage than all the things in the past put together," he said.

"My brother S. William says they're moving in mining machinery above Lucy's Liver."

"I know," he said quietly. "Have you ever seen a place that's been strip mined?"

She shook her head.

"It's a woeful sight. Looks like a great tornado passed through." He paused. "I can't rightly describe it, but I can show you. There's a place up here where you can see what it's like."

He started up the slope. She knew that she should be leaving, but she was intrigued. If this sight had made such an impression on him, it must be worth seeing, she persuaded herself. And with everyone talking about stripping, she ought to know what it was. She followed him once again.

"Sometimes when I look across at Green Pine Mountain, I just know I couldn't let that happen here. I'd die first."

The intensity of his words surprised her. He seemed to be making an awful fuss over digging out a little coal. And giving your life to stop it was going pretty far. But she wasn't worried because her kinfolk would never let it happen in her hollow.

They entered the thickest woods she'd ever been in. Without a guide, she would have been lost in a few minutes. But the boy had no trouble locating a trace that wound its way up the mountain and eventually came out on top of the ridge. Once there, Dan'el found an open spot where they could look across the wide valley to the mountain beyond.

Fair Annie gasped when she saw it. After the lushness of these hills, the stark nakedness of Green Pine came as a shock. Its very name was a cruel joke. Barren and rock-strewn, the mountain showed no sign of life—no trees, no grass, no flowers. Even the birds seemed to avoid it.

Halfway down its side was the remnant of a cabin, mashed under a tremendous landslide that had uprooted the remaining trees and left them lying at crazy angles, like jackstraws. Near the top of the mountain were gashes where erosion had eaten deep gullies and spit out the soil in the creek below; it was thick with mud.

"They augured coal in there. I saw them do it," Dan'el said as he pointed to the dark seam that ran along the cut. Large holes had been bored into the seam every few feet.

"They had a machine with a drill this big." He formed a large circle with his hands. "It just chewed back into the coal like it was hard candy, and the trucks hauled it away."

"I think it was better when they dug down underground for the coal."

"But this way's cheaper, and that's what counts . . . at least with the Axel Coal Company. Why pay men to dig when the machines can just cut off the top of a mountain? They had one machine that was as tall as that oak." He indicated a tree about thirty feet tall. "The mountain's dead now," he lamented. "Nothing will grow on it again."

She had to agree. It was dead. The shattered cabin was the only evidence it had ever supported life. Fair Annie felt depressed and almost physically ill after taking in the destruction.

"Didn't mean to make you feel so bad," Dan'el said. "But I feel the same way, because that could happen anywhere there's coal." He threw back his shoulders and tried to look cheerful. "Well, no use us acting like mourners. We can't do anything about Green Pine. All we can do is try to keep the stripping from coming closer. Do your folks know what they're up against?"

Fair Annie considered. "S. William's worried, and that's unusual. He's always wearing the bells; never takes anything seriously. But he seems to understand about some things better than the others. I . . . I think he goes outside the hollow . . ." She left the sentence unfinished.

Dan'el nodded but made no comment. After a pause, he said, "Have you told your pappy about Blue's Son?"

"Law, no!" she replied quickly. "I'd get strapped good if he knew I was here."

"Most folks stay clear of 'the wild McFarrs.' " He spoke with a mixture of pride and sarcasm.

"And nobody wants to tangle with 'all them Collinses,'" she said.

They looked at each other and burst out laughing. It was the first time she'd ever heard him laugh—a strange, choking sound, beginning in his throat and emerging as a chuckle. Probably the best he could do with so little practice, she thought. She began to feel a rapport with this boy, an understanding that she'd never shared with anyone before, not even Molly Vaughn or Barbara Allen—and least of all, Otis. There'd been no feeling like this between them. This was so different, it puzzled her. She wasn't sure what to make of it.

They started back down the slope, working their way through the groves of sourwood and poplar, giant oak and beech, and over rough boulders that had rolled down from the upper ridges. Dan'el was undaunted by the terrain, but now and then he stopped to extend a hand to help her over a particularly difficult spot or to point out a new clump of wildflowers that caught his attention.

"Wood sorrel," he'd say simply, pointing to a stand of little white flowers. Or "Solomonseal," indicating the slender, green-belled plants thriving in the sun-flecked shade. The same flowers grew in Old Mule Hollow, but she didn't know them by these names. Sometimes she made up her own names for them.

They didn't converse much, she and Dan'el, but he seemed to smile a little more often. She was beginning to find his piercing eyes less threatening, his black brows and hacked-off hair less strange. She was no longer afraid of him.

Suddenly a roar worse than thunder split the quiet of the forest, followed by the crash of falling trees.

Dan'el looked stricken. "They've started!" he said.

chapter six

Fair Annie didn't understand.

"The mining machines. The Axel Coal Company's started stripping," Dan'el explained. "Old Woman had a notice some time ago that they were going to mine a seam along Juniper Mountain and that she'd have to move. Her house is in the way."

"But it's *her* house!"

"Doesn't make any difference. The coal company owns the mineral rights, and that gives them the say-so over everything. Grandpap McFarr told me that the company bought up the rights way back. They paid about twenty-five cents an acre for them, and the mountain people were glad to get it. But most of them couldn't read or write and didn't understand what they were giving away."

The noise came from the direction of Juniper Mountain all right—just where S. William had said the machinery was moving in. Dan'el stood quite still, listening. Then he started walking again, not down the mountain as they'd come, but parallel with the ridge. Fair Annie had no choice but to go along. She'd never find her way back alone.

After covering some difficult ground, they reached an area where great boulders had piled up. By standing on them, they could see across to Possum Gap. Old Woman's cabin looked undisturbed. The machinery that was making all the racket was out of sight, farther down the ridge behind the trees.

"I aim to find out if she's all right. You can wait here. I won't be long."

Fair Annie remembered the elderly woman's kindness in providing medicine for Blue's Son. The least she could do now was to try to help her if she could. Without explaining, she followed Dan'el. He turned, as if he'd expected her to come, but he asked no questions.

She was constantly surprised that he seemed to understand her feelings. In that respect he was completely unlike any of the boys she'd known. They were seldom at ease with girls the way they were with other boys, but were always teasing and joking—a sort of verbal wrestling match to show that they were in charge. But Dan'el treated her as an equal, something unheard of in Old Mule Hollow. And she liked it.

They seemed to climb for an interminable amount of time before she realized that it was the roar of the machinery, not the distance, that was making it so difficult. The thud of crashing trees and the scraping of metal on stone was nerve-racking. Fair Annie tried to hold her hands over her ears, but she couldn't keep her balance while climbing that way. Old Woman must be in misery, she thought, with all that noise so close by.

They found the woman sitting disconsolately in the rocker on her tilted porch. Her dogs, frightened by the din, gave only halfhearted barks at their approach. From here the mining machines were visible in the distance. They looked incredibly big. One orange monster with a shovel on one end was pushing everything in its path over the side of the mountain—soil, trees, rocks. The sight of ancient trees being ripped out, roots and all, was almost more than Fair Annie could bear. She turned and faced Old Woman.

"I knew you younguns was comin'," the elderly woman said, rousing herself to welcome them courteously. "I'm afraid I'm too woeful to be worth visitin' today. I have a mort of trouble."

"Maybe we can help," Dan'el suggested.

"Thankee kindly," said the woman, "but I'm beginnin' to think that no one can help. I've prayed and prayed, and not even the Good Lord's been able to stop those infernal machines. They're the Devil's own work, and that's the truth!"

"Have the company men been here again?"

"Oh, they was here, all right! Said the same thing as afore: that I'd have to leave so's they could peel off the top of this old mountain. I tol' 'em they'd have to peel me off with hit, cause I ain't a-movin'. Unless hit's to join my Maker. And that's the truth, too."

"They show no mercy when there's coal around," said Dan'el. "You'd best move out, Old Woman. They'll clean you off of here without a prick of conscience."

Old Woman set her feet. "I ain't a–movin'! I declare, hit benasties the mind to think there are men like that—so all-fired greedy they'd tear down the gates of heaven if they thought there was ary bit of coal there. But they'll fry in hell, and that's a fact! Almost makes me want to go there jes' to see hit."

"You could come home with me," Fair Annie found herself saying. "My generations will put you up." She knew only too well that the Collinses didn't welcome strangers, but this was different. Old Woman wasn't an outsider; she was one of them. And the Axel Coal Company was the common enemy.

"I'm kindly obliged, but that wouldn't save my cabin," Old Woman told her. "I'm a-goin' to take a stand. Right is right, and nobody can gainsay that."

Dan'el hesitated. "My folks have been . . . making plans. I can't say anymore than that right now; it's better you don't know. But meantime, maybe Pap can talk to the men . . . put them off. I'll go ask him."

They left Old Woman still seated on her porch, her pack of mongrel dogs lying close by. The gloom and despair shrouding the scene was as thick as the dust settling on what was left of the green beauty of Juniper Mountain.

"Do you think your pa can help?" Fair Annie asked.

"He'll try, I'm certain. Some of the workmen are mountain men themselves. They'll listen, but they can't do much or they'll lose their jobs. It's the company that's to blame. The people who run it don't live around here. Most of them live up North—Philadelphia, places like that. They never see this land that makes them rich. If they had to use the red water in Great Day Creek, or got burned by the acid in Delaney Branch, things might be different."

Fair Annie realized more than ever why hope was in such short supply in the hollows. Things always seemed to be stacked against the highlanders; they couldn't win. Until this moment, she hadn't fully understood her urge to leave the hills. Now she knew that it wasn't for clothes and boyfriends, as she'd thought, it was to escape. If she stayed, she'd live next door to despair all her life, like the rest of her kin people, and she didn't want that. Rooming with Patty Ruth Ann might be a high price to pay for a new life, but it would be worth it. She really had no alternative.

Dan'el was descending the slope rapidly now, and she had trouble keeping up. His face was grim, and he seemed unaware that she was falling behind.

Then, unexpectedly, he turned and waited. His face relaxed and he looked slightly amused at her awkwardness in working her way down with bare feet. But his expression quickly changed to concern when a sharp stone made her wince. Dan'el didn't have her foot problem; he wore boots. They were too large and, undoubtedly, had seen at least one former owner, but he wore them proudly and they protected his feet.

She had just caught up with him when a shot rang out above the sound of machinery. It seemed to come from Possum Gap. They stared at each other, sharing the same dreadful thought.

"It wasn't a rifle," he muttered, almost to himself, and she knew what he meant. Mountain men used rifles or shotguns. Anything else meant an outsider.

They hadn't traveled far from the place where they'd looked across to Possum Gap. Now they backtracked, and in a few minutes they were standing on the great boulders, studying the scene over at Old Woman's cabin. They could see two men in the front yard. One of them held a smoking gun.

On the ground nearby was a bundle of clothing. It looked . . . With a sudden surge of horror, Fair Annie realized that the bundle was Old Woman!

chapter seven

Dan'el reached Possum Gap long before Fair Annie got there. The men with the gun were gone, but Old Woman was still on the ground. Fair Annie had to make herself look. Then the bundle moved! Old Woman wasn't dead; she was kneeling beside one of her dogs that lay stretched out in the grass. It had been shot in the head.

The woman was the picture of misery as she knelt over the dog. She didn't cry, but mourned in the way mountain women often do, with a long, low wail of anguish.

"He only tried to protec' me," she told Dan'el. "Didn't do nothin' 'cept growl when they hollered at me because I hadn't moved out. Old Bige was a mighty fine dawg, no better on earth. I wisht they'd a-shot me an' been done with hit."

Fair Annie sensed movement around her. When she looked toward the mountainside that she and Dan'el had just traveled, she saw a very tall, straight man emerge from the woods and stand watching, as if appraising the situation. In a moment another appeared, and then another, all coming from different directions and as stealthily as shadows. She could see that they were lean and alert, with the same piercing eyes as Dan'el. These had to be wild McFarrs—three of them. With rifles! And she, a Collins, right in their midst.

One of the three, a middle-aged man, came forward. His face was lined and weather-beaten, the face of a man who'd spent most of his life out-of-doors. And while the others were very tall, this one was a giant. Almost seven feet, she guessed. As the man approached, Dan'el stood up and regarded him with respect. But Fair Annie drew back in fear.

The man studied Old Woman as she continued to mourn her dog. The rest of her pack had retreated under the porch and were peering out nervously.

Nodding toward the woman, the man said, "Take care of her, boy." Then he gave Fair Annie a long, penetrating look but said nothing to her.

"All right, Pap," Dan'el replied.

In a few minutes all three men had vanished as swiftly as they'd come.

"You'd best leave for a spell," Dan'el advised Old Woman. "You can share our cabin."

The little hollow-eyed woman got up, wearing the resigned expression that Fair Annie had seen so often on highland women. "I dasn't stay for their sakes," she said, motioning toward the dogs. "Law! They'll shoot 'em all jes' for meanness. Bige didn't do nary thing but what any dawg worth his salt would do. And they shot him. They was tryin' to scare me, I know, but that didn't give 'em the right to do that." She sighed deeply. "Well, looks like them machines has won."

The woman went to her cabin, still railing against the men who'd killed her Bige. Fair Annie went along to help her pack. Before going inside, she looked back and saw Dan'el burying the dog at the edge of the woods.

Old Woman took a worn quilt from her bed and spread it on the table. Then she filled it with packets of the herbs and dried plants she used in her medicines. Next to the dogs, these seemed to be her most cherished possessions. After adding a few pieces of worn clothing and several pots and pans to the collection, she got down on her knees and pulled a box from under the bed. In it was a black cotton dress and a large piece of white satin, carefully folded.

"My buryin' dress and satin to line my box," she said. "I want to look gaily when I leave this world. And I want a fair amount of preachin' over me. I been aimin' to ast the preacher man to do hit, but I hain't seen him in a whet. Cain't git to church anymore."

It didn't take long to gather together her meager belongings. Dan'el came in and packed some food in a box—a few jars of "sass," pieces of dried pumpkin, and "leather breeches" that had been hanging on strings from the rafters. Finally he added a little smoked meat that Old Woman must have been given in exchange for medicine. When they were ready to go, he slung the cornhusk mattress over his shoulder, balanced the front porch rocker on top, and that was it. All of the worldly goods of a lifetime carried by three people.

Before starting off, Old Woman said, "I'm kindly obliged to you, Dan'el, but I'll not be goin' to yore cabin. The dawgs might not git along with yourn and . . . Well, I'm used to doin' fur myself. I'll jes' stay in that cave yonder til things git settled one way or t'other. If'n my cabin goes, I kin move into an empty place some'ers. Goodness knows there's plenty of 'em now."

Dan'el started to protest, but the woman wouldn't hear of any change in her plans. "My mind's made up. I'd be plumb miser'ble if'n I was a burden to folks."

It wasn't until they began the descent from Possum Gap that Fair Annie and Dan'el realized exactly what they'd undertaken. In spite of her independence, Old Woman was terribly frail. No one knew how old she was; she wasn't too sure herself. But they could see now that scrambling over the rough terrain, even with their help, was beyond her strength.

With the pack of dogs at their heels, Fair Annie and Dan'el attempted to keep her between them for support as they slowly inched their way down the mountain. At this rate the descent would take a week, and there was always the risk that the woman would fall or die of exhaustion.

Dan'el soon stopped, put down his load, and took stock. Without a word, he removed the rope from one of the bundles and after arranging and rearranging it, managed to tie the rocker to his back. Fortunately his slim hips fit easily between the rockers that extended before him.

He knelt down and Old Woman, with Fair Annie's help, sat down in the rocker. When he stood up, she gave a loud hoot as she was lifted into the air on Dan'el's back. She clung tightly to her swaying perch, while the dogs pranced and yapped, uncertain how to react to Old Woman's flight.

Even with the chair on his back, Dan'el was able to carry the box of food in his arms, and Fair Annie lugged the quilt full of articles. But a few of the things, including the mattress, had to be left behind. Dan'el assured Old Woman that he'd come back for them later.

As the little procession made its slow, tortuous way down the mountainside, Old Woman gradually relaxed and began to enjoy her new mode of transportation.

"Dan'el Boy, nary mule ever carried me better'n this. Yore a pure credit to yore kin. And that's the truth! Law, this is the way to travel!"

By the time they reached the cave, Fair Annie was so tired she was ready to drop. And Dan'el, too, looked weary as he put down his passenger. He lit the candle in the cave, and Blue's Son began to whine when Fair Annie entered.

"So this is the dawg that thought it could handle a bar," said Old Woman as she began examining his wounds. "Needs more of my sab, but hit's doin' fine. Don't you worry, Fair Annie. I'll take good care of yore crittur. My dawgs won't bother him none. I'll see to that."

The sun was already dropping behind the mountains, leaving long, purple shadows to mourn the day.

"Hit's too late for you to be traipsin' round the hills after my other stuff. I'll make do with what I got," Old Woman told Dan'el.

"I'll get them tomorrow," he promised. Then they helped Old Woman arrange her quilt on the bale of straw and left. For all her lively talk, she was tired and needed rest.

Fair Annie quickly started for home, afraid that darkness would catch her in these dense woods. She expected Dan'el to head homeward, also, but he came with her.

"I'll see you to the ridge," he said. "The dark's coming fast, and you could get turned around in here."

As they walked along, Fair Annie remembered a question she'd been wanting to ask. "I know one of those men at Possum Gap was your pa, but who were the others? I was sure they'd want to know who I was."

"Those were my uncles. They wouldn't question you with Pappy there. If he didn't ask any questions, that meant there weren't any that needed to be asked. I haven't told him about you and your dog yet, but he usually knows what's happening on our land. I guess we all do. We can sort of smell something different."

This didn't strike Fair Annie as odd. Her kin operated

the same way. They could tell when a stranger was around almost before they saw him. Even she could tell, although she couldn't explain how.

The shadows lengthened and the woods became quite dark. Fair Annie was afraid. This was eerie territory, even in daylight, with wild McFarrs all around . . . maybe watching down their gun barrels. She was sure they could see in the dark with those sharp eyes. Anyway, Dan'el didn't seem to be having any trouble. Then she realized that the same thing was true of her. She could find her way around Old Mule Hollow anytime of the day or night.

The boy reached out and took her hand. He had an uncanny way of reading her mind.

"I don't want us to get separated until you're on familiar ground," he explained.

Fair Annie rested her hand in his strong, callused one and marveled at the comfort and pleasure it gave. When she and Otis played dominoes, their hands touched occasionally, but it never made her feel joyful, the way she felt now. It wasn't a foot-tapping, fiddle-playing kind of joy, but something quieter: more like a slow melody, drawing her closer to the boy beside her. Suddenly she wanted to laugh at the joke played on her. Here she'd been praying for a pretty young man, and the mountains had delivered a shaggy-haired, fierce-eyed McFarr. Yet she had no regrets.

They came to the ridge overlooking her valley. Logging and farming made the woods sparse here, and night turned back to twilight. Dan'el stopped at the boundary of his land—out of habit or caution, she wasn't sure which. But either way, it was ironic. She'd trespassed, and the McFarrs had done nothing. But if Dan'el set foot in Old Mule Hollow, there wasn't a Collins alive, except maybe Lord Randal, who wouldn't take a shot at him.

They stood for a minute on the ridge as the evening mist swirled around them, leaving fine beads of moisture on their hair. Slowly the mountains vanished into the mist. They were alone at the top of the world.

"Good night, Fair Annie," Dan'el said softly. His words touched her like a tender caress.

"Good night, Dan'el," she replied, and knew that she would remember this moment forever.

chapter eight

Fair Annie floated down the slope and across the swinging bridge over Old Mule Creek. Just hours ago, it seemed, she'd been ready to leave the hollow. It offered nothing but hardship and misery; even the land was doomed. Now the hardship was still there, but also a bubbling of hope. She could look forward to tomorrow . . . and the day after, something she'd never done before. But she knew that she was playing a dangerous game. If Pa found out . . .

She was halfway up the hillside when she was startled to hear music. That sounded like Uncle Druxter playing his guitar. And Aunt Tot on the fiddle.

As she drew closer to the cabin, she heard the unmistakable shuffle of a square dance—a play party! But why tonight? And a weekday, too? For a few seconds of panic, she thought that she might be in the wrong hollow. Maybe she'd gone all the way to Wednesday Fork. She checked around her and knew that there was no mistake. That was her cabin. And those were her kinfolks, clapping and stomping to the dancingest tunes they knew.

She went around to the back door. Some of the men were there, sampling Uncle Ben's latest batch of whiskey—"white lightning," they called it—which he made in a secret still high up in the mountain. So far, the government men who sometimes came looking for illegal stills hadn't found it. Fair Annie remembered that once she'd tasted a drop of the stuff and it was awful! Even nastier than the spring tonic Ma made the family take every year "to clean out the blood."

She moved, unnoticed, into the crowded cabin. The bed had been pushed against one wall and the chairs against the other, leaving room in the center of the floor for the dancing. Jugs of cider were on the kitchen table, along with a bag of pretzels and popcorn. These were undoubtedly contributions from relatives who were drawing welfare. It was the custom for everyone to bring refreshments to a party; but at this time of year, before the crops came in, supplies were always low and only those receiving welfare had anything extra to contribute.

Also on the table was a cracked plate filled with taffy, the kind Ma made in the big iron skillet. She cooked it until it turned black and hard as nails, then cracked it into pieces with a hammer. With patient sucking, it softened and became chewy. Fair Annie could see that Nancy Belle had helped herself generously to the taffy. She had such a big glob in her mouth, her jaws were stuck together and she couldn't speak. Mollie Vaughn and Jimmy were teasing her about it.

Uncle Partee's voice and the final do-si-do finished together. He stopped, wiped his forehead, and took a drink of cider. The dancers also crowded around for refreshments. Fair Annie still didn't understand the reason for this celebration. No one had said a word about it earlier, unless she'd been so busy worrying about getting back to Rancey Hollow that she hadn't heard. But it didn't seem possible that she'd miss anything as important as a party. They hadn't had one for months—not since February when Uncle Bangs had a party and games just to relieve the long winter boredom.

Barbara Allen looked especially happy. And so did Billy, as he stood beside her at the back of the room.

"I didn't know about all this," Fair Annie whispered to her. "Did someone get an extra welfare check?"

Barbara Allen laughed and shook her head. "Law, if you ain't the limit! Billy and me up and decided to git married. Since he's been drafted, at least he'll git paid regular." She looked up at the blonde, stocky boy beside her. "I still cain't believe hit. We're gittin' married Saturday mornin'. Billy has to leave on Monday, so Preacher Barclay's comin' out special to marry us. Mr. Wells called him on the store telephone."

Barbara Allen turned her attention back to Fair Annie.

"Say, you've been gone almost the endurin' day. Where you been?"

"It wasn't so long," Fair Annie countered. "Did anyone miss me?"

"I doubt hit. We've all been gittin' ready for the party right hard—except Patty Ruth Ann. As soon as she saw work to do, she took off to visit her folks til we was done."

Fair Annie glanced across the room and saw that her cousin had cornered Otis again. The poor boy was putty in her hands, smiling like a simpleton every time she looked at him.

Fair Annie said to her sister and Billy, "I wish you both happiness, I kindly do." There was a time when she might have been jealous of such happiness. But she understood her sister's feelings better now and was glad for her.

Energetic Aunt Tot bounced in from the kitchen and claimed attention by banging on the metal dishpan she carried.

"Time for candy-breakin'," she announced and began snapping sticks of colored candy into pieces and placing them in the dishpan. Then she covered the whole thing with a towel.

"The guests of honor first," she said, pulling Barbara Allen and Billy forward. Barbara Allen dutifully stuck a hand under the towel, fished around in the dishpan, and drew out a fragment of red candy. Billy reached in and withdrew a yellow piece.

There was a chorus of "aw's" because they hadn't drawn the same color and had to put the candy back. But this bit of bad luck had no effect on their beaming faces.

Nancy Belle and Uncle Partee's girl, Cally, rushed forward to be next, but Mollie Vaughn intercepted them. "Mind your manners and let your elders go first," she told them firmly. They grudgingly obeyed.

Mollie Vaughn and Jimmy then took a turn, with the same results. One had a red piece of candy, the other green, so they couldn't keep them.

Fair Annie noticed S. William across the room, looking at her rather intently. She hadn't seen him until now and had assumed that he was behind the house sampling the contents of Uncle Ben's jug. He wasn't supposed to touch whiskey, but S. William was never a great one for doing what he was supposed to.

Now she watched in surprise as he spoke to Otis and escorted him across the room.

"Otis, here, aims to git himself a piece of that candy," said S. William, "and he thinks yore jes' the one to help him. Don't you, Otis?"

Otis looked dazed, as if he wasn't sure what had happened to him. Fair Annie suspected that S. William was up to something, only she didn't know what. But he didn't miss much, and that worried her.

"We're purely lucky, Otis," her brother added offhandedly. "We got the prettiest women in the country right here in this holler. Nothin' like kinfolks."

Otis resigned himself to giving up Patty Ruth Ann temporarily and went with Fair Annie to the dishpan. Nancy Belle and Cally were there again, and this time they succeeded in getting a turn. They squealed with delight when each drew out a piece of green candy. Nancy

Belle immediately crammed hers into her mouth, which wasn't easy to do, since she was still working on the large wad of taffy.

Fair Annie and Otis took their turn, but drew different colors. She thought it was a further sign that they weren't a match.

The candy-breaking ended with the last scraps being handed out as Great Aunt Eula brought in a basket of little muffins that she called "cakes."

"For the younguns," she said out of habit. Since going on welfare, she had enough flour and sugar to make cakes for the young and old alike. And no play party was complete without a fortune-telling from her baking.

"Here's yore future in a cake," she cried, making her chins shake. Great Aunt Eula enjoyed her own cooking and, unlike the other women in the hollow who ranged from thin to skinny, she'd grown quite round, especially since she'd started receiving welfare. "A sack of flour tied in the middle," was the way Pa described her.

Once again Nancy Belle was first in line and managed to escape Mollie Vaughn's attention. Great Aunt Eula blindfolded her before letting her select a cake.

"Break it open and see what you got," her aunt said. Everyone knew that three objects had been baked in the cakes: a ring, a penny, and a thimble—symbols of things to come.

Nancy Belle was beside herself with glee when she found the "ring," actually a metal washer, in her cake. This meant that she would marry soon. She put the washer on her finger and waved it about for all to see.

When Mollie Vaughn and Jimmy opened their cakes, she had nothing, but he had the penny, a sign that he'd be rich someday. He grinned a little sheepishly.

"Reckon I won't have to worry about a job now," he said. "I'll jes' set back and wait for the money to roll in." Everyone laughed, but the laughter was tinged with sympathy. They understood how it was with him.

"That's quare," said Great Aunt Eula, checking the cakes. "There oughta be a thimble amongst you."

Fair Annie had been watching the others and had forgotten the cake in her hand. Now she broke it open and there it was—an acorn cap, the substitute for a real thimble. But the meaning was the same: She was going to be an old maid. Her kin all teased her, because no one doubted that she'd marry someday, in spite of the unmerciful amount of schooling Pa insisted on. Fair Annie laughed good-naturedly but kept thinking about the forbidden path her heart was taking.

Since the musicians were still eating cakes and not ready to tune up again, there were calls for Grandpa Collins to tell a story—"about Aunt Coot." He had a fund of stories about their aunt, who had been an eccentric even by Collins standards.

Grandpa's long, solemn face wore the faintest suggestion of a smile as he surveyed his audience with satisfaction. He'd been patiently waiting for this request.

"Some of you younguns might not know 'bout yore Aunt Coot . . . I reckon she be yore great, great aunt by now . . . so maybe I oughta explain 'bout her. She was a little woman, no more'n five foot, but wiry. And strong-willed! Whooo-eee! I tell you she was! She told everybody what to do and when to do hit. And if'n she didn't git her way, she'd do the durndest things.

"But I recollect one time she didn't git her way. Hit was at Betty Joe's weddin'. Betty Joe was her favorite niece, so when she said she was gittin' married as soon as possible, cause her Jack was goin' in the Army—same as Barbara Allen and Billy here—why Aunt Coot said they'd have to wait til she finished butcherin' her hogs so's she could hold a nice weddin' fur 'em at her cabin.

"Now Betty Joe's ma wasn't a Collins—only a kin by marriage. She'd been a Miller from over in Delaney Holler, and she'd had enough of Aunt Coot's bossin'. Besides, she had six girls to marry off, and she didn't want to give Jack time to change his mind. So she said Betty Joe was gonna git married at home and went ahead with the weddin' plans.

"When the kinfolks arrived, Aunt Coot was still sayin' the weddin' would be at her house next week. But Betty Joe's ma was jes' as stubborn and said they was holdin' the weddin' then and there.

"Well, Aunt Coot stretched out on the floor and kicked her heels up and down, sayin' they warn't. Hit was a sight, I'll tell you! There they was, preacher an' all, tryin' to have a weddin', and there was Aunt Coot on the floor kickin' and screamin'—and her nigh onto eighty years old. Law!

"Finally Uncle Shadrach come. He was her brother and the onliest one that could handle Aunt Coot. He tried to pick her up, but she jes' stiffened herself out like a board.

She could do that right good, stiffen herself out. Well, Shadrach picked her up and carried her like a stick of wood.

"Now they'd been a-diggin' out a stump in the front yard, right next to the fence, and hadn't filled in the hole yet. So Shadrach jes' planted Aunt Coot in that hole . . . stood her in there, still stiff. 'Bout that time Uncle Clyde come along and he couldn't see too good, nohow, and he called out to Betty Joe's daddy, 'Mighty fancy fence post you got hyear, Tom.' We like to split from laughin'.

"Aunt Coot got so mad, standin' in the hole with everybody laughin', she finally climbed out. And she didn't make nary a bit more fuss 'bout the weddin', cause Uncle Shadrach kept an eye on her and she was afraid he'd plant her in the hole agin. Shadrach died not long after that, and Aunt Coot said hit was a sign that she'd been right and he shouldn't of interfered. After that she did the contrariest things, jes' to git her own way. Did 'em til she went to her reward, or wherever she went. Next time we git together, I'll tell you what happened when that social worker lady called on Aunt Coot."

Most everyone already knew, and they laughed just thinking about it.

The music started up and Uncle Partee, fortified with food and drink, was again the caller for the dance:

"Raise the window, raise it high
Your own true love is passin' by . . ."

Nancy Belle suddenly screamed. She had brushed her

arm against the hot stove in the kitchen. A fire had been kept burning in it to take the chill off the cabin and to heat the big coffee pot. Great Grandma Collins, who'd been a burn blower most of her life, immediately went to work. She held the girl's arm out and examined the reddening patch on the elbow.

"Have to git the fire out," she said quietly, as large teardrops rolled down Nancy Belle's nose. Grandma murmured something to herself, then passed her hand over the burn three times, blowing on it with each pass. After the third time, the skin looked less red.

"Fire's all out, I think," she said. Nancy Belle sniffed and said it didn't hurt now. This was no more than expected because Grandma had healed the burns of several generations and still hadn't lost her power.

While everyone crowded around to observe the burn-blowing, Fair Annie saw S. William, Lord Randal, and several other young men go outside. By the light from the kitchen window she could see them gathered under an oak tree beside the cabin, having a serious discussion about something. She suspected it was the strip mining. The subject hadn't been brought up openly during the party, but she'd heard enough low-voiced comments to know that it was very much on everyone's mind.

Fair Annie watched from the window, wishing that she could join them. Now that she'd seen stripping with her own eyes, she couldn't forget it. And try as she might, she couldn't wipe out the memory of Old Woman mourning her dog. But she knew that if she did join the men, they'd change the subject until she left. Women took care of the home, the children, and some of the farm work; anything beyond that was a man's world. But for all their talk, Fair Annie didn't think there was a thing the men could do against the power of the coal companies and those great machines.

The party was ending, and Uncle Druxter suggested a final song to honor the bride-to-be. What could be more appropriate than all nineteen verses of the ballad that had provided her name? Everyone joined in to sing:

"T'was in the merry month of May,
The green buds, they were swellin',
Sweet Billy courted a fair young maid;
Her name was Barbara Allen . . ."

chapter nine

In spite of her long day and the party, Fair Annie had trouble getting to sleep. While Mollie Vaughn, Patty Ruth Ann, and Nancy Belle breathed rhythmically beside her, she clung to the edge of the bed, wide awake. She seldom had trouble sleeping. In fact, she couldn't recall that it had ever happened before.

Perhaps she was too tired to sleep. All that scrambling up and down mountains had worn her out. As she lay there, mentally leafing through the events of the day, she lingered over her journey home with Dan'el. She could almost feel the falling mist, her hand in his. But why was she getting so soft-headed over a McFarr, of all people? She could find no answer, and it remained a mystery.

She finally dozed off and was just settling into sleep when a distant rumble rattled the window. She got up quietly and leaned over Barbara Allen's bed to look out. Somewhere in the direction of Juniper Mountain, a great ball of light suddenly leaped into the air and burst into a million scarlet pieces—just like the fireworks that Mr. Wells sometimes shot off at Christmas. Only this wasn't Christmas. Almost at the same time, flames jumped higher than the treetops, turning the black sky sunset red. A big fire was raging back in the mountains, but this valley was too deep and the trees too tall for her to tell exactly where. She was sure, though, that it was far enough from Old Mule not to be a threat.

She was tempted to awaken her sisters, to show them the brilliant sky, but changed her mind. They were sleeping peacefully and hadn't stirred. She'd probably have missed it, too, if she hadn't been unusually restless.

Fair Annie shivered in the damp air and crept back to bed. The noise she'd heard must have been thunder, she concluded. A storm was brewing, and lightning had set the fire. Such blazes happened all the time but seldom spread because the woods were dripping with dew.

She fell into an uneasy sleep that made her waken at the slightest sound. Toward dawn, she heard a window open slowly. She sat up, listening. The wall between the two bedrooms was paper thin, and she could tell that the sound came from next door—her brothers' room. The window closed again. It had to be the boys because she could hear them whispering and moving around. In a moment, the cornhusk mattress rustled, followed almost immediately by the slightly musical whistle that S. William made when he slept.

She lay down and wondered if they were just getting in. With S. William, anything was possible. Maybe he'd traveled farther than usual to visit a girlfriend. But not Lord Randal. He wouldn't visit anyone except Betty Lou, and he'd never get in to see her at this hour. Her folks kept her on a tight rein.

In the morning Fair Annie was as tired as if she'd been shucking corn all night. And it didn't make her feel any better to see Patty Ruth Ann and Nancy Belle hop out of bed, fresh and rested. Mollie Vaughn and Barbara Allen were always slow to wake up, and for once she could understand how they felt.

Pa was an early riser and had always insisted that her brothers follow his example. But this morning he let them sleep and didn't call them until he'd finished breakfast. When they finally got up, they were unusually quiet. Fair Annie could sense tension in the air.

She made her regular trek to the barn and pigpen to feed the animals, wondering how much longer she could safely delay telling Pa that one of the piglets was missing. But first she had to get Blue's Son home; that would be one less thing to explain. She decided to get him today, if he was well enough. Old Woman would probably be glad to get him out of her way while she was living in the cave.

Fair Annie had secreted a chunk of cornbread for the dog in her pocket. Also a bit of fatback that she'd scooped out of the leftover beans Ma had stored "outdoors," meaning the unheated pantry off the kitchen. They had no refrigerator.

By the time Fair Annie finished her chores, the sun had penetrated the valley and the mist was gone. She could see Pa and the boys plowing on the hillside, which meant that they could also see her. She'd have to be very careful or her trip to Rancey Hollow would end before it started. She was trying not to look forward to going back and reminded herself that this was strictly business. She might as well face the fact that there was no place for a McFarr in the future of any Collins. The line dividing the families was wide and deep, and any attempt to bridge it might shatter the fragile peace that now existed.

While the men were busy prying out a stone, Fair Annie ran down the rough slope, her bare feet suffering the consequences. Once in the dense woods, she felt safer, but only from being seen by her kin. She was still nervous about becoming a possible target for the McFarrs.

As she went deeper into the alien land, she was aware of something different. She couldn't quite put her finger on what it was and kept listening. She could hear the chirping of birds, the sound of the creek . . . That was it! She could hear all the sounds of nature again. They weren't drowned out by the roar of machinery as they'd been yesterday. She hoped this meant that the miners had packed up and gone away, but she doubted that was the case.

Now she caught a glimpse of the rocks where Dan'el

would be waiting. She could picture him standing there, tall and still, blending in with the forest so well that only a sharp eye could pick him out.

But when she reached the rocks, he wasn't there. She whistled several times, but he didn't come. After waiting impatiently, she decided that she'd have to go on alone. Or go home. Only that would be hard on Old Woman because she didn't have any food to spare for Blue's Son. She barely had enough for herself. Her own dogs must be foraging for their meals.

Fair Annie wasn't at all sure that she could find the cave again. The woods were dense and confusing, and she was used to having Dan'el lead the way. She took a chance and began to climb.

It bothered her that Dan'el wasn't here. Maybe she'd taken too much for granted. He could be tired of guiding her around. Suddenly she saw the rock outcropping. The cave should be just about here . . .

A sharp whistle startled her. It seemed to come from farther up the slope. Through an open space among the trees, she could see someone waving. It was Dan'el. As she climbed toward him, it became apparent that she'd completely missed the cave.

"I'm glad I saw you before you wandered too far," Dan'el said. She thought he sounded relieved. "I've been checking out a cabin for Old Woman and just got back."

They continued to the correct rocky mass and circled around to the hidden entrance. There they found Old Woman sitting outside the cave, feeding her dogs scraps of food from a limp paper sack. Blue's Son was enjoying the handouts, too, and Fair Annie was amazed at how much better he seemed.

"I'm sorry you had to feed him," she said. "I'm late bringing his food."

"Hit don't matter," Old Woman replied. "Jes' as easy to feed 'em all to once. My dogs ain't used to huntin' fur their meals. Didn't catch nothin' but a dead squirrel." She took Fair Annie's meat and cornbread and stuffed it into her bag. "I hope yore both right gaily this morning."

"I'm feeling pert," Dan'el told her. "And I've got good news for you. Pap says you can live in Uncle John's cabin. He's in Detroit now, and I doubt if he'll be back. It's farther down the hollow, near the mouth of Rancey Creek. It'll be easier for you to get about there. But the cabin's not in very good shape. I'll clean it out today so you can move in, and patch it up later."

"That's purely a pleasure to hear," said Old Woman. "A cave hain't the same as a home. You are a credit to yore folks, Danny Boy." She looked up toward Possum Gap. "I was jes' settin' here thinkin' and wonderin' if them coal people can sleep nights, with all that on their conscience . . . ruinin' God's handwork and throwin' old women out of their homes. Hit don't seem like they should git nary a bit of peace for a-doin' that."

"The company's getting money, and that's all they care about," Dan'el replied.

The old lady nodded in agreement. "I reckon yore right."

"Can you find your way back?" Dan'el asked Fair Annie. "I want to clean up the cabin so I can get Old Woman moved before dark."

"I'll help you," she volunteered. The words just seemed to pop out, and then she was reluctant to withdraw the offer.

Dan'el slowly developed a smile. "I could stand some help, and that's a fact. Never was much at house cleaning."

Without another word, he left; Fair Annie went behind him down the rocky slope toward Rancey Creek. She shivered as she saw that they were going farther away from Old Mule Hollow and deeper into enemy territory.

"You sure your folks won't shoot a Collins on sight?"

He gave his strange chuckle. "Don't worry. If they intended to shoot, you wouldn't be walking here now."

She found that less than reassuring. "But if they know I'm a Collins . . ."

"The McFarrs may be 'wild,' but they aren't stupid. They don't shoot without good reason. Of course, now, if some of your menfolk started coming here to hunt or something, they might get a warning shot past their ear."

They stopped in front of a cabin overgrown with weeds and vines. Obviously it hadn't been lived in for a long time. But it was an improvement over the cave or Old Woman's home at Possum Gap.

"With a little fixing up, it shouldn't be too bad," said Dan'el.

They tore away a tangle of honeysuckle and Virginia

creeper that had taken over the porch steps, and went into the musty-smelling cabin. Several pieces of furniture had been left behind by Dan'el's uncle—an old sofa, complete with a mouse nest in one battered cushion; a table; and a homemade chair, still sturdy though its seat of woven cornhusks was almost gone. Dust and cobwebs covered everything.

"Looks bad now, because it's so dirty," Dan'el said, "but it can be fixed up." He brought in a twig broom and mop from a shedlike kitchen tacked on the rear of the cabin and opened the windows.

Fair Annie didn't feel too hopeful about its possibilities, but she grabbed the broom and attacked the piles of acorns, sticks, and corncobs left by the most recent inhabitants—the four-footed ones. Dan'el gathered up bottles, boxes, and other debris and threw them outside.

At home she'd have done anything possible to get out of a job like this, she thought. Yet here it was a challenge: just the two of them trying to make a home for a nice old lady.

After working awhile, Dan'el pulled a package from his pocket. It contained a thick sandwich. She realized then that she was hungry. According to the sun, it was noon, dinnertime. He gave her half the sandwich, and they sat outside on the old porch to eat. She felt completely at peace here. The discontent was gone. It was a happy time, and she savored it all the more because there'd been so few of them.

When they went to work again, she found herself

humming as she swept—an old riddle-song she'd heard all her life. Dan'el joined in with the words and they both began to sing:

> *"I gave my love a cherry without a stone.*
> *I gave my love a chicken without a bone.*
> *I gave my love a ring without an end . . ."*

Suddenly the clang and thunder of machinery left the song unfinished. They stood still, recognizing the noise and all that it meant. The stripping of the mountain had been forgotten for the moment, but now it cast a chill over the cabin.

The natural sounds of the forest ceased, lost in the man-made din. Fair Annie tried to remember the way it had been just a few minutes before: the soft sigh of the wind, the songs of birds, the raucous call of a crow—sounds that seemed more precious now that they were gone.

"The company's brought in *more* machines," Dan'el stated. She read a deeper meaning behind the words and suddenly thought of the red sky.

"That fire . . . over on Juniper Mountain! That was the machinery?"

He nodded. "Blown sky-high. A beautiful sight!"

She knew better than to ask who did it.

"I'll tell you one thing," he replied to the unasked question. "This stripping's got people riled up for sure, and more than one clan's joined in to stop it. Anger's still running mighty strong over what happened to Mr. Benson. The coal companies can't keep stomping on people like bugs, just because they happen to be in their way."

Fair Annie recalled hearing something about a Benson . . . oh, yes, the preacher had prayed for one of them last Sunday. But she hadn't paid much attention. She'd been more interested in dreaming about a pretty young man who'd rescue her from the hollow someday and provide her with an endless supply of ruffled dresses. How childish that seemed now!

"What happened to Mr. Benson?"

"When the miners started tearing up his farm, he threw himself in front of a bulldozer. So a deputy sheriff shot him. The judge didn't do a thing to the deputy. Said he was only doing his duty and let him go free."

The ruined cabin on Green Pine Mountain flashed through her mind and she felt great sympathy for Mr. Benson.

"Before this ends, there'll be more machines blown up, and probably more people killed," Dan'el predicted.

They tackled the cleaning with renewed vigor to wipe out their troubled thoughts. As if on cue, they both began singing again, this time loud enough to drown out the machinery and the groan of the protesting mountain:

"A cherry when it's bloomin', it has no stone.
A chicken when it's pippin', it has no bone.
A ring when it's rollin', it has . . ."

Fair Annie stopped suddenly. "Listen!" She thought she heard voices outside.

Just then there was a loud knock on the open door that rattled its loose hinges. They stepped to the doorway and faced a man in a tan uniform standing on the porch. Other uniformed men stood around the cabin, hands resting on gunbelts.

"Your name McFarr?" the man asked.

Dan'el murmured, "Yes."

The man turned to the others. "Well, boys, what do you think of that? We've caught us a gen-u-wine wild McFarr!"

chapter ten

"We have a few questions to ask you about the damage to Axel Coal Company equipment," the uniformed man said to Dan'el in a tone of authority. "You'd better come along with us. We need to talk to your folks, too. What's the best way to get up yonder?"

Dan'el said nothing.

"It might go easier with you if you cooperated. We only want some information. Just doing our job, you know." His voice became less stern as he tried to cajole Dan'el into helping them. "Now show us the way, and we'll show you how grateful we are."

"I'm afraid I can't do that," Dan'el replied, and the man looked at him suspiciously.

"Did you say your name was McFarr?"

"Yes, sir."

"Well, you sure in blazes don't sound like no hillbilly."

Until now, they had ignored her, and Fair Annie hoped they wouldn't ask her name. They'd never believe that she was a Collins.

The man who seemed to be in charge inclined his head in her direction. "What about her?" he asked.

"She's just visiting . . . doesn't know her way around," Dan'el told him.

"O.K., boys, take him back to the car. And don't say I didn't give you a chance to help yourself, McFarr."

Fair Annie stepped forward to protest, but the boy gave her an almost inperceptible shake of his head. She kept quiet, for fear of doing more harm than good.

Two of the men led Dan'el away, and the others continued along Rancey Creek. None of them looked very eager to enter this dark valley that was home to the unpredictable McFarrs. Even the man in charge kept glancing over his shoulder. Fair Annie, watching from the cabin, thought they had a bad case of "the allovers."

As soon as they'd gone she started up the hillside, hoping that Old Woman would know where Dan'el's father was. She dreaded facing him, but he'd have to be told about his son—if the men hadn't arrested him, too.

The cave wasn't far from Rancey Creek, she remembered. It shouldn't be too hard to locate from this direction. She searched for the faint path she and Dan'el had followed that morning and finally found it. But it faded away occasionally, and she had to retrace her steps several times before she heard the bark of dogs and knew that she was close. After circling the rocks, she found Old Woman still sitting outside the cave.

"How's my cabin comin' along?" she asked.

"Something terrible's happened," Fair Annie said, and plunged right into the story of Dan'el's arrest.

Old Woman kept her watery eyes glued on Fair Annie during the whole recital. Then she wiped a hand across her face and shook her head. "That coal company's got a lot to answer fur. They're headed straight fur the hot place. Poor Dan'el! What he needs is a good lawyer man to stand up fur him. But they want an arm an' a leg jes' to say howdy, and he don't have two nickels to rub together. We'll jes' have to pray for Dan'el. And I'll tell his pappy. He'll be here with some victuals afore long. But you git home and warn yore folks. The law might be aimin' to clean out yore holler as well as this 'un. But leave yore dawg. He ain't up to fast travel yet."

"I'm sorry we didn't get you moved. And I'll be back as soon as I can to take Blue's Son off your hands."

"Don't worry none 'bout that. Me and him's friends. Now you go lickety-split across the ridge."

Fair Annie went as fast as she possibly could, but even though she'd made this journey before, she wasn't sure that she was taking the right route. She had no way of knowing that she wasn't headed for a deep gully or a sheer rock face that would be impossible to cross. As she walked, she looked for familiar landmarks, but the dense woods were most confusing. She hoped they were just as confusing for the lawmen.

Her main goal was to climb the ridge above her. Once on top, she could get her bearings more easily. After a long, hard pull up the slope, she finally looked down on Old Mule Creek and could scarcely believe her good luck. She was almost opposite her family's farm!

She had just started across the bridge over the creek when she caught sight of Uncle Druxter, puffing and panting up the dirt road and carrying a bag. Apparently he'd come from Wells's store.

"Boys! Boys!" he shouted when he saw Pa and her brothers plowing the hillside. "Come quick! I got news!"

Without waiting for them to get closer, he shouted, "They're comin' . . . down yonder." He pointed down the road. "I lit a shuck fur home soon's I heard, but they ain't fur behin'."

"Who ain't fur behin'?" Pa wanted to know.

"Sheriff. And a whole pack of deputies. Nasty-lookin' critturs. Ol' Man Wells told me they're spoilin' fur a fight. The coal company's so riled up 'bout the fire, they went an' complained all the way to the govner. Now they's arrestin' everybody they kin find. Only want to question us, they say, but I don't trust nary one of 'em."

He had continued up the road while he was talking and was now so far away that they could barely hear the last sentence. It was obvious that he didn't intend to be around when the sheriff and his men came along. But he'd make sure that the news spread. They could hear his special holler echo through the valley to alert their kin.

Pa and the boys dropped their tools and headed into the woods. Experience had taught them that the law was always on the side of the expensive lawyer man, and the coal companies kept well supplied with those. The uneducated highlanders didn't have a chance against them.

Fair Annie couldn't risk being seen by the law again, so she waited behind a tree. Soon she saw what she'd been expecting—men in tan uniforms with guns at their sides. Like Uncle Druxter said, the coal company must really be riled up to have the law coming in force into places they seldom entered and usually avoided. The people in the hollows always settled their own problems and called on the law only as a last resort.

She could see the men round the curve near Grandpa's house. He was leaning against a porch post, watching them.

"Your name Collins?" the man in the lead called out.

Grandpa sent a fine stream of brown tobacco juice from the side of his mouth before replying: "Hit might be."

"Know anything about that explosion up on Juniper Mountain?"

The old man rubbed his chin as a breeze ruffled his white hair. "Didn't hear no give-out 'bout hit," he said vaguely, as if he wasn't sure of anything.

The law shrugged in exasperation and mumbled, "C'mon," to the men. As they came up the road opposite her hiding place, she had a clear view of the man who seemed to be in charge—a big man with a stomach that lapped over his belt buckle.

"No use wasting time on that old geezer," he said. "We'll clap a bunch of these hillbillies in jail, then you'll hear 'em talk. They'll sing like birds, I'll guarantee you!" He gave a coarse laugh and the others smiled. But they all looked as nervous about going into Old Mule as those who'd entered Rancey Hollow.

When they were out of sight, Fair Annie crossed the creek and made her way up the hillside to the pigpen. Everything seemed in good shape there, so she started toward the house. But she got no farther than the barn before Patty Ruth Ann appeared suddenly, almost beside her. Where had she come from this time, Fair Annie wondered. She hadn't noticed her until this minute.

Her cousin narrowed her eyes and said, "You're acting mighty queer, Fair Annie. That's the second time I've seen you crossing the creek from the other side. What're you up to, anyway?"

"Nothing. And I can go where I please without explaining to you!" She was in no mood to put up with a cross-examination from Patty Ruth Ann. Kin or no kin, there was a limit.

"Your pa might like to know where you've been. Especially if you're meeting somebody down by the creek. He'll have a few things to say about that." She wore a smug look that Fair Annie found most irritating. But at the same time, she was glad that the girl didn't know the truth. If Patty Ruth Ann wanted to believe that she was meeting someone by the creek, that was all right with her.

"When are you going to ask your father about leaving?"

"I haven't said I'd go yet."

"But you haven't said you wouldn't. Besides, I think you're too smart to stay here and have nothing, when you could go outside and have plenty of everything—clothes, food, boyfriends. You know you're not going to pass that up. So tell Uncle Ned and get it over with. He'll let you go."

She swaggered off, leaving Fair Annie furious. As if she cared about such things when people were being arrested! It was a good thing Bertha and Flossie weren't like that or she wouldn't even consider moving in with them. But they'd always been more Collins than Brown and kept Patty Ruth Ann in her place.

"Did you see your pa or the boys?" Ma asked anxiously as soon as Fair Annie entered the cabin. "The law's been here askin' questions."

"We played the dumb hillbilly and they left," Mollie Vaughn interjected with a laugh. "Any Collins that ain't smarter than that sheriff deserves to be caught."

"I saw Pa and the boys go off in the woods," Fair Annie said. "Uncle Druxter sent out word."

Ma nodded in approval. "I hope they don't find nary a soul. They look like trouble to me."

The girls had been preparing for Barbara Allen's wedding on Saturday by cleaning the cabin. That was about all the preparation they could afford. But the bride-to-be didn't seem to mind as she happily cleaned the grease and smoke from the kitchen window.

Aunt Nestor dropped by to contribute a jug of cider for the wedding celebration. Ma put it on the floor in the corner of the cabin, where there were already several other jugs, gifts from around the hollow.

"Hit might wet a few throats," her aunt said modestly. "Bangs wuz goin' to bring it 'round, but he got wind of that posse and went off. I reckon Ned and your boys lit out, too."

"They be gone. Them coal people! Won't be satisfied til they tar and feather somebody. And all the endurin' time they're tearin' up folks' homes with their big machines. Hit jes' don't seem right, but the govermint won't lissen to nobody but them fellers."

Darkness was coming on quickly, and Aunt Nestor rose to leave while she could still see the path. Just then Pa and the boys came into the house.

"I'm right proud to see you back, Ned," said Aunt Nestor. "Did you chase that posse out of the holler?"

"They chased theirselves out. Never seed sech a bunch of durn fools. Me and the boys follered 'em right up the crick. Watched 'em from the woods and they never knowed hit. By the time they got to Here We Come Branch, they give up. Couldn't find a man person nowheres. So they went back where they come from. We heerd some others was in Rancey Holler, lookin' fur McFarrs. Think they caught one."

Fair Annie thought that S. William gave her a quick glance but decided that he meant nothing by it. She must be feeling guilty about her secret visits there.

"Bangs was with us, Nestor," Pa said. "He's gone home now."

"Well, I'll git on home, too," their aunt replied.

Pa began regaling the family with the details of their adventure with the law. The boys took over when he paused for breath, and the wonder of it grew with each telling. The girls listened, always appreciative of a good story.

But Fair Annie had stopped listening at the mention of the McFarrs and started thinking again about Dan'el's fate. If Old Woman hadn't told his father, she'd just have to risk trying to find him herself.

They ate their supper of coffee and cornbread, with a little of the cheese that Ma made regularly from milk supplied by their nannygoats. Then Pa took down his banjo and started to play. He was in such a good humor after outwitting the government men that he didn't stop playing until they'd sung seventeen verses of "A Frog He Went A-Courting." As customary, the singing ended with a hymn, this time "Amazing Grace," and the family went to bed.

Fair Annie fell into an exhausted sleep. It seemed that she'd been in bed only a few minutes when she heard a knock on the door. A heavy, gray mist covered the window, so she knew that it must be dawn—but early, because neither Pa nor her brothers were up yet. The knock came again. Then the front door, which was never locked, banged open.

"Don't reach for your gun," a gruff voice said. "Just get up and get dressed. You're under arrest."

chapter eleven

All of the girls were awake now, peering around the bedroom door. Fair Annie recognized the uniformed man who stood inside the cabin entrance. He was the one with the sagging stomach, the one who'd been searching the hollow yesterday. Two more men entered from the kitchen. Not only were they wearing guns at their sides, but they were carrying rifles as well.

They opened the door of her brothers' room and ordered the boys to get dressed. Then one of them pushed against the girls' door, but their screams made him back off.

"What's this all about?" Pa thundered as he rolled out of bed and stood in his underwear facing the officer.

"I think you know already. You Collinses live by your own laws and get away with it most of the time. But when a coal company gets a million dollars' worth of machinery damaged because you don't like what it's doing, that's something else. Now you've got to answer to the law of the land. So let's go!"

Without further explanation and with barely time to dress, her brothers and father were handcuffed and shoved out the door. Fair Annie heard one officer mutter apologetically to Lord Randal, "It's part of the job. I do it or get fired." He was a mountain man, and these arrests rubbed against the grain. Fair Annie might have felt sorry for him if she hadn't been so bitter about the whole business.

Ma and the girls got dressed and heated coffee to keep warm. The men were gone and they were suddenly faced with a void of leadership. No one knew what to do. Although they sometimes resented being bossed by the men, they still depended on them for decisions.

"We could go talk to Uncle Druxter and some of the others," Barbara Allen suggested. Then she gasped. "Maybe they've *all* been arrested! Even Billy!"

"I wonder if they got my brothers?" Patty Ruth Ann said, as if this thought hadn't occurred to her before. She put on her coat and hurried out. Yesterday none of them had been too concerned, confident that the law would never catch the men. But they hadn't anticipated this raid.

Now they could hear talking and shouting nearby. Fair

Annie and her sisters rushed to the front porch. The mist still shrouded the road, but they recognized voices. That was Uncle Druxter sounding off, there was no doubt about it. And there were others, coming down the mountain road. Apparently the officers had made quite a catch. As the voices faded, Fair Annie thought that she heard Otis.

"Well, hit looks like there's nary a thing we can do," Ma said with a resigned sigh. She had the deep conviction that the laws of the outside were beyond comprehension and any mountaineer caught breaking them was doomed.

"We can't sit here and do nothing until they're ready to let the men go. Might be years!" Mollie Vaughn protested.

"Maybe Mr. Wells would know what to do," Barbara Allen suggested. "If he ain't arrested, too."

Since yesterday, when Dan'el had been picked up, an idea had been forming in the back of Fair Annie's mind. She felt hesitant about mentioning it, but it seemed to be their only hope.

"What we need is a good lawyer," she told them. "Everybody says the law won't listen unless you have a lawyer speaking for you." They stared at her in surprise.

Then Mollie Vaughn spoke up: "Yeah! And we also need about a hundred dollars. That's what them lawyer men cost. Where're we goin' to git that much money?"

Fair Annie pressed on. "We know a lawyer—Mr. Armour, the man Pa brought home to hear us sing. He told Pa to let him know if he could help him at any time. Well, now's the time."

"He was jes' bein' polite. People say things like that without really meanin' hit," Barbara Allen explained gently.

"Anyway, he's in Burlsville and that's a fur piece—more'n twenty miles away," Mollie Vaughn added. "Nary one of us ever been farther'n Wells Lick, so how're we goin' to git there?"

These were questions Fair Annie had already asked herself. Finding Mr. Armour wouldn't be easy, and there was a good chance he'd turn them down. A big-town lawyer would be awfully busy, probably too busy to return a favor. Still, he'd impressed her as a man of his word.

"We could find him if we tried," she persisted. "We have to!"

Ma shook her head. She didn't believe in asking favors of anyone, least of all an outsider. "Law! You cain't count on folks out yonder to help you. That's a careless world out there, that's what hit is. I went there oncet and they wouldn't give you the time of day."

Barbara Allen said, "No use runnin' off on wild goose chases, Sister. Sooner or later we'll find an answer right here in the holler. Meanwhile we ought to do the men's work around here, or Pa'll be right put out when he gits back."

Everyone was visibly relieved to be back on more familiar ground.

"Well, I reckon!" Ma said. "You two help me finish plantin' the corn," she said to Mollie Vaughn and Barbara

Allen. "Nancy Belle, git them dishes done and straighten up in here. And you," she motioned to Fair Annie, "take care of the stock, like common, then come holp us in the field."

The girls sprang into action and seemed glad to be dealing with farm chores instead of trying to cope with the law. But Fair Annie couldn't put the problem aside. The coal company wanted revenge and had enough power to get what it wanted; everyone knew that. The only way the police could protect themselves was to round up some likely culprits, whether they were guilty or not. After all, who was going to prove they weren't? And a McFarr would have the least chance of all. Tales about them were legendary. People would believe the worst.

By the time she'd fed the pigs, her mind was made up. She didn't know exactly how she'd manage it, but she was going to talk to Mr. Armour. She considered asking Mr. Wells to telephone him, then rejected the idea. It would be too hard to explain over the phone, and he might say "no" right off. She had to talk to him face-to-face, tell him about the arrests. And it was important for him to understand that she wasn't asking for something for nothing. Pa wouldn't allow that. She didn't have money, but she could offer other things—maybe quilts for his family. She'd heard that outsiders were beginning to prize handmade ones. And Lord Randal could make him a "dulcimore," and . . . There were lots of things they could give him. And if that wasn't enough, she'd clean and scrub for the Armours until the debt was paid.

Fair Annie felt almost lighthearted now that she'd figured out the payment. She rushed through feeding the goats and cow so quickly, they were too skittish to eat.

While Ma and the girls were in the cornfield on the hillside, Fair Annie slipped into the cabin to find the card that Mr. Armour had given her father. She was afraid that Nancy Belle would get nosey, but luckily she was banging pans and singing so loudly that she didn't hear her come in.

Fair Annie went directly to a tin mug on a shelf beside her parents' bed. This was where Pa kept important things, like chewing tobacco and shotgun shells. She emptied the mug, and there was the card: JAMES R. ARMOUR, ATTORNEY AT LAW, 123 HIGH STREET. That was her passport, she hoped, to a world she'd never seen before. Right now it seemed as remote as another planet.

She passed up the dirt road for the woods, so that Ma and her sisters wouldn't see her and forbid her to go. Unmindful of damage to her feet, she alternately ran and walked to Wells Lick. There was no time to lose. She was counting on Mr. Wells's knowing the direction of Burlsville, because she had no idea where it was.

The men who hung around the store for lack of something better to do hadn't arrived when she entered, and there were no other customers.

"Howdy, Fair Annie," Mr. Wells said, glancing up from his account books. Then he quickly asked, "Did they get your menfolks? I wished I'd seen 'em in time to warn your generations, but they come up here long before I opened the store. I heard 'em, though, even if I couldn't scarcely see 'em because of the mist and all. Don't know how they found their way. I expected 'em to stop here, but they kept right on up the road."

"They came to our house for Pa and my brothers before we were out of bed."

Mr. Wells shook his head in dismay. "Makes you wonder what things are comin' to. Reminds me of them Nazis in Germany. I was over there during the war, you know. But I never thought we'd have anything like that here. It's them coal companies. Got politicians and the govermint sewed up in their pockets. Well, I'm sure sorry to hear about your folks. Anything I can do for you?"

Fair Annie handed him the card. "I'm going to see Mr. Armour—the man who called on us last Sunday. He's a lawyer. But I don't know how to get to Burlsville."

Mr. Wells closed his account book and gave her his full attention.

"Now let's see if I have this straight. You're plannin' on goin' all the way to Burlsville to pay a call on that lawyer man?"

Fair Annie nodded. "He told Pa that if he needed him, to let him know. So I'm going to ask him to help get the men out of jail." She paused. "Maybe he won't do it, but it won't hurt to ask."

Mr. Wells pursed his lips in thought. "I reckon it won't," he conceded. "But that's a mighty big jaunt, Fair Annie. You never been beyond the holler, have you?"

"No, sir, but I aim to go now. You have to have a lawyer to deal with the law. Everyone says so."

"You're right there. A mountain man doesn't have

much chance even *with* a lawyer. Tell you what. Mr. Pitt oughta be along in a few minutes with the mail. Welfare checks come today. He'll be headin' in that direction, and maybe he'll give you a lift. I sure hope that lawyer feller'll help you. It's an endurin' shame fur men to have to stand by and let a company mess up their land. Like that old sayin', 'The rich get richer while the poor get poorer.' "

He reached under the counter and brought out a licorice whip. "Here. Have a treat while you're waitin'."

Fair Annie thanked him and appreciated his kindness. She was beginning to feel terribly nervous about traveling so far. And by herself. She wished one of her sisters had come with her, but they'd made it clear that they thought the whole idea was crazy.

She fidgeted around the store, finally settling down before the big Sears Roebuck catalog that Mr. Wells kept in the back. She turned to the blue gingham dress with all the ruffles that she looked at and admired each time she came here. But today it didn't impress her. It was only a dress, and she had far more important things on her mind.

She heard the cough of Mr. Pitt's jeep. Then the short, red-faced man who'd been conquering mountain roads for many years sang out, "Mailman!"

"Mornin', Mr. Pitt," said Mr. Wells. "You've got a load today, I see."

"Yep. Welfare checks mostly. Seems like I carry more of these checks each time I come."

Fair Annie waited patiently for this ritual of exchanges to be completed. Then Mr. Wells said, "This here's Fair

Annie Collins from Old Mule Holler. She has some important business in Burlsville. Think you could give her a ride?"

"Nope, sorry," Mr. Pitt said. "It's against government regulations to carry passengers. What's so important in Burlsville?"

"Well, it's an emergency, and that's a fact. You hear about all the arrests over sabotage of Axel Coal Company equipment?"

"Yeah. They've been talking about it all along my route. Nasty business, arresting people on sight. They got some Browns, I hear, but nary a McFarr, except one boy."

"Well, her folks is in jail, too, and she knows a lawyer feller that might get 'em out."

Mr. Pitt considered the request again. "Maybe I can take her as far as the main highway. I know nobody up here's going to report it if they see her in my jeep. But I can't risk carrying her into town."

"What about it?" Mr. Wells asked Fair Annie. "It's still a mighty long walk to Burlsville once you get to the highway." Before she could reply, he turned back to Mr. Pitt. "She ain't used to traffic. Never been out of the holler." They continued to discuss her journey as if she weren't there.

Finally Mr. Pitt had an idea. "My brother lives just off the highway. He has a small contracting business—does a lot of work in Burlsville. If I could use your phone, Mr. Wells, I'll give him a call and see if he can take her."

He returned from the phone with a triumphant smile on his red face. "We're in luck! He's going into town to give an estimate on a job . . . says he'll take the little girl."

"That's mighty kind of you, Pitt. If that lawyer manages to get the folks out of jail, I'll tell 'em they can thank you for helping out."

Mr. Pitt beamed and escorted Fair Annie to the jeep, after first depositing the mail with Mr. Wells, who was also the postmaster. The roads into most of the hollows were too rough for cars or completely blocked with trees and boulders, so this was as far as mail delivery went. The residents had to pick it up at the store, where they usually left behind a good portion of their welfare checks, since this was the only place around to spend them.

"Big day for folks in the hollers . . . for Mr. Wells, too. He'll get what's owed to him," Mr. Pitt commented as they started down the rutted road. Fair Annie grasped the edges of the seat and held on for dear life. She'd never ridden anything that didn't have four legs, and certainly nothing that went as fast as this machine on wheels. It was terrifying! But she tried not to let her fear show.

"Your family on welfare?" Mr. Pitt asked.

"No, sir. Pa won't hear of it. He farms as best he can."

Mr. Pitt raised his brows and looked at her with interest. "You think this lawyer can get your kin out of jail?"

"I don't know, but the coal company uses lawyers to get what it wants, so we ought to be able to do the same thing."

Mr. Pitt gave a nod of agreement. "You've got a point there."

The rough road made talking difficult. Mr. Pitt had to swerve the jeep from side to side to avoid the deepest ruts, and Fair Annie's fingers ached as she tightened her grip on the seat. After many miles, the road smoothed out. The dirt turned to gravel, and eventually the gravel became hard, black paving. Fair Annie had never seen a road like it. But she was even more amazed when it joined a highway that had a strip of grass growing right down the middle. It was so wide, four rows of cars could use it at the same time!

"Slide down in the seat a little," said Mr. Pitt, "so no one will notice you. I'm bending the rules by carrying you. But, as Mr. Wells said, this is an emergency. Those coal companies need to be taken down a peg or two, and I hope that lawyer can do it. Well, here's my brother's place."

They had turned off the highway and were driving up a short lane to a neat, brick house. Compared to the shacks in the hollow, this one looked like a mansion to Fair Annie. She thought that the Pitts must be awfully rich to live here.

The brother was loading some tools into the back of a truck when they arrived. "Howdy, Vernon," he called to Mr. Pitt. "This the little girl?"

The mailman introduced her to Byrd, his brother. After hurriedly explaining why she needed to get to Burlsville, he went off to complete his rounds.

"You just made it," said Byrd, as red-faced and jovial as his brother. "I got an appointment and can't afford to be late, so climb aboard."

He drove down the lane carefully, then suddenly took off on the highway as if something was chasing him. Fair Annie clung to the seat and shut her eyes. She'd been afraid before, but now she was almost beyond fear. She couldn't believe that anything could move this rapidly. Whenever she dared open her eyes a little, she saw the roadside flashing by in a blur as the wide road went on and on with scarcely a bump or curve. She began to feel sick and wished she hadn't come.

"Well, now, what's this lawyer's name and where's his office?" Mr. Pitt asked.

Fair Annie gulped and tried to relax enough to answer. "He's Mr. Armour—one, two, three, High Street."

"Armour. Yeah, I've heard of him. Supposed to be a pretty good lawyer. Sure hope he can help you out." He glanced over at her and asked, "This the first time you've been out of the hills?"

She moved her head; that was easier than trying to speak. Mr. Pitt laughed. "I thought so. Everything comes as a shock, I guess. Well, let me tell you something, Annie. You may find a lot of fancy things in town—hot water, electric ice boxes, big houses—but you have something that money can't buy. Look at that!"

She saw him wave a hand toward the green mountains, then quickly closed her eyes again. "Peace. That's what you've got up there. You won't find that down here in this rat race. No, sir. When I retire, I'm going to find me a little place on a mountaintop and stay there."

Mr. Pitt slowed down as they reached the edge of town, and she risked looking around. To her surprise, she saw a light dangling right over the road. It was green. Then as they approached, it turned red. Mr. Pitt stopped the truck, but she didn't know why, unless he wanted her to get out here.

The man looked at her, and seemed to understand. "That's a traffic light," he explained. "Tells you when to stop and go."

The cars crossing the road in front of them stopped now as the light turned green again. Mr. Pitt shifted gears and drove on. "You're going to find a lot of new things that'll be mighty confusing, but you'll get used to them before long."

He turned a corner and drove more slowly. "This here's High Street. And there's the building you wanted—one twenty-three. Just go right in and ask someone where Mr. Armour's office is. If I had the time, I'd stay and help you, but I can't afford to lose this job."

He stopped the truck in front of a tall building—almost as tall as a mountain, Fair Annie thought. She could see rows of windows, one on top of the other. Six of them, going up into the sky! She'd read about such buildings, but she'd never seen anything taller than the one-story cabins at home.

When she got out of the truck, the ground beneath her feet felt cold and hard. There wasn't a blade of grass anywhere, only a sea of gray concrete covering everything.

"If that lawyer sends you packing, just wait for me right here," Mr. Pitt told her. "I'll be back along about five. If you're here, I'll carry you home and you can spend the night with my family. Vernon can take you back tomorrow when he delivers the mail. Good luck, now!"

Before she could thank him properly, he drove off, muttering something about his appointment. Fair Annie bent her head back to look up at the towering building. It didn't appear very inviting, but at least she'd made it this far. If her luck held, she'd find Mr. Armour in there.

Several people turned to stare at her. She glanced down at her tattered dress and bare feet and understood why. She looked completely out of place among the well-dressed folks going into the building. She felt ashamed of her appearance and wished she could escape back to the hills.

Then she thought of Pa and her brothers . . . and Dan'el. She shouldn't be concerned about looks at a time like this, she scolded herself.

Fair Annie straightened her shoulders and marched resolutely into one twenty-three.

chapter twelve

Fair Annie was puzzled to find only a big room when she entered the building. Where were the offices? Then she spotted a large sign with many names on it. Among them was: JAMES R. ARMOUR, ATTORNEY AT LAW, 6 FL. That must mean sixth floor, the top of this stacked building.

She tried to figure out how to get up there. The front door seemed to be the only way in or out, but there wasn't any way up—unless it was through that little room at the back. It was about as big as their pantry at home, and as she watched, people kept going into it and vanishing! As soon as they entered, the doors closed and a green light on the wall lit up. In a few minutes a red light came on, the doors opened again, and different people came out. Purely magic!

A plump, motherly looking woman came over and asked if she needed any help.

"I'd like to get up there," Fair Annie said, pointing toward the ceiling.

"There's a stairway in back, or you can take the elevator," the woman explained. "Come with me." She gently steered Fair Annie into the little room and asked, "What floor did you want?"

"Sixth, please," Fair Annie replied, not quite knowing what to expect.

"That's my floor, too," the woman said, and pressed a button with a large "6" on it. Immediately the doors closed and the little room seemed to glide upward, but so smoothly that she wasn't really sure that they had moved. Suddenly the doors opened again, all by themselves.

"Here we are. Now move along quickly!" The woman propelled her out of the room. And just in time. The doors zoomed shut right behind them. Another second and they'd have been squashed!

"Think you can find your way now?" the woman asked.

Fair Annie, still unnerved by the elevator, glanced down the hall. On a door straight ahead, she saw Armour. "Oh, yes, thank you." she said with relief. "I'm going right there."

The woman gave her a kindly nod and moved on. Fair Annie decided that her family had a lot to learn about outsiders. So far, they'd all been extremely nice to her.

She stood before Mr. Armour's door. The top part seemed to be glass, only it was all frosted up and she couldn't see through it, so she timidly rapped on the wooden frame.

No one answered. If Mr. Armour wasn't there, she didn't know what she'd do. She hadn't considered that possibility. She rapped a little harder.

A young woman about the age of Barbara Allen, but not half as pretty, opened the door. She appeared surprised to find Fair Annie standing there.

"I *thought* I heard a noise. Were you knocking?"

Fair Annie said, "Yes, ma'am."

The girl looked her over and asked coldly, "Well, what do you want?"

"I'd like to see Mr. Armour, please."

"You have an appointment?"

Fair Annie shook her head.

The girl looked annoyed. "Do you know Mr. Armour?"

"Yes . . ." The ma'am sprang automatically to her lips, but she swallowed it in protest. This girl was deliberately making things harder. Fair Annie reached into her pocket and produced the card Mr. Armour had given her father.

The girl glanced at it, then said reluctantly, "Come in. Sit down over there." When Fair Annie started to sit on the light beige sofa, the girl said quickly, "Not there; over there," indicating a dark brown chair.

Fair Annie was embarrassed, knowing that the girl thought she was too dirty to sit on the sofa.

"Mr. Armour's busy. I'll tell him you're here in a few minutes." The girl sat down at her desk and began fingering a machine as if she were playing a piano. Only no music came out.

Fair Annie watched, fascinated. She remembered reading about a machine like this—a typewriter! That's what it must be. She was dying to ask how it worked, but didn't dare. The girl had already made it plain that she considered her a nuisance, and Fair Annie suspected that she was just waiting for an opportunity to throw her out.

When the girl glanced her way, Fair Annie self-consciously tucked her bare feet under the chair and sat stiffly on its edge. She didn't want to do anything to hurt her chances of seeing the lawyer.

A door at the side of the room opened unexpectedly, and a man strode out. It was Mr. Armour! He handed the girl some papers without noticing Fair Annie. She waited tensely for the girl to tell him she was there, but the girl said nothing. She didn't know what to do, because Mr. Armour was closing the door again. Then he happened to look in her direction.

"Why, you're one of the Collins girls!" he exclaimed in surprise. He turned to the girl at the desk and said sharply, "You should have told me she was here, Miss Brandt." While Miss Brandt sputtered an excuse, he invited Fair Annie into his office.

"I hope you haven't been waiting long. Sometimes my secretary tries too hard to protect me. Now, let's see, you're Barbara Allen?"

"No, sir. Fair Annie."

"Ah, yes! 'Fair Annie of Roch Royal.' I think that was a fine idea your parents had, naming you all after old ballads. I kind of wish my folks had thought of it. They could have named me 'Billy Boy,' or 'Old Dan Tucker.' " He laughed. "With a name like that, nobody in court would ever forget me."

Fair Annie laughed with him and felt much more relaxed. It occurred to her that that was what he was trying to do—put her at ease before getting down to the business of her visit. A smart man, this Mr. Armour.

"Now what brings you out of the mountains and all the way to Burlsville?" he asked pleasantly.

She swallowed a few times, trying to remember what she'd planned to say. "You told Pa if he ever needed help, to let you know." She hesitated before going on. "I wasn't sure whether you really meant it . . . you must be awfully busy . . . but he sure could use some help right now."

"What's happened?"

"Pa and my brothers and some other kin people were arrested this morning. The lawmen came into our cabin before we were out of bed and took them away. They said they just wanted to ask questions about the Axel Coal Company's equipment. It was blown up, over on Juniper Mountain where the company's strip mining. They're tearing the top right off of old Juniper and . . ."

She stopped, reminding herself to be brief. With a fancy office like this, he couldn't afford to waste time.

"Yes, I know about strip mining." She thought that he looked angry. "I've represented some conservation groups in legal action to stop that particular type of destruction, but the courts invariably rule in favor of the coal companies."

"It doesn't seem right to tear up land like that," Fair Annie said.

"It isn't right. And it's a black page in history that's allowed it to go on through the years. You see, this isn't something new. It really goes back to the eighteen hundreds, when the coal companies sent their agents out into the hills and got the settlers to sign long, complicated deeds, selling their mineral rights for a few cents an acre. The people signed, mostly with an 'X' because they couldn't read or write, and they didn't understand that they were giving the companies the right to do whatever they wanted to get the coal out. It wasn't so bad when most of the mining was underground, since it provided jobs and didn't change the surface too much. But these new machines that take the coal from the top are simply ruining the land." He stopped and unclenched his fists. It was obvious that he had strong feelings on the subject.

"I'm afraid I get carried away when I talk about stripping, and I know you didn't come here for a lecture. Let me ask you this, did the officers who came to your home have any sort of papers with them . . . a warrant?"

"No, sir. They just took our menfolk away. And some others in the hollow, but I don't know exactly who. I didn't have time to find out before I left."

"I see. Well, I appreciate your faith in me, but don't expect miracles. However, I have a feeling that this is another one of the sheriff's high-handed operations, and he may have overstepped his authority this time. I'll be glad to see what I can do."

Fair Annie was jubilant. The longer she talked to Mr.

Armour, the stronger her confidence in him became. Then she quickly raised the point that was the hardest to express, but she had to let him know that she didn't expect charity.

"I know you must charge a lot, with this fine office and all. . . . We can't pay you in money, but we can pay in other ways. We'll make you quilts, and a dulcimore, and . . ."

Mr. Armour held up a hand to stop her. "Forget the quilts, or dulcimer, or anything else. I've already been paid for my services. Your family took Gene and me into your home, and you sang some songs that I've been trying to collect for years. You don't owe me a thing. Now, I'd better get over to the sheriff's office and find out what sort of charges he's trumped up against your folks. You go home and . . ." He looked at her. "How did you get here, anyway?"

She told him about the rides with the two Mr. Pitts, and Byrd Pitt's offer to let her stay overnight.

"But what would you have done if you hadn't been lucky enough to find someone to drive you?"

"I'd have walked," she said without hesitation.

Mr. Armour shook his head. "Your mother must be worried about you, so you'd better not wait for this Mr. Pitt."

He opened another door, and she could see into a small room lined with books. There, seated at a table and surrounded by books, was Gene. His father said, "Here's our friend from Old Mule Hollow. You remember Fair Annie."

"How could I forget?" Gene said as he joined them. "Hi, Annie."

Mr. Armour told Gene about the arrests. "I think the sheriff's trying to make points with the Axel Coal Company. They were very generous to him during his last election campaign." He handed Gene some keys. "Take Fair Annie home while I see about getting her people released."

"Sure thing!" Gene replied. "Come on, Annie, before he changes his mind and makes me take my old wreck. I don't get a chance to drive the family wheels very often."

Fair Annie thanked Mr. Armour again. But there was one other thing she had to say before leaving, although it embarrassed her to ask for more.

"If it isn't too much trouble . . . one of the McFarrs was arrested, too . . ."

Mr. Armour laughed. "I'll see what I can do about the lot."

She felt reassured. If anyone could help, he was the one. With Gene by her side, Fair Annie walked confidently into the little room with the magic doors. She didn't even mind too much when people turned to stare. She couldn't blame them, really. Her ragged dress and bare feet made a strange contrast with Gene's appearance. Even in jeans and a faded shirt, he looked better dressed than anyone in Old Mule Hollow.

He took her to a car, the big blue one the Armours had driven to Wells Lick the previous Sunday. Everything inside was also blue, and the seat was so sleek and smooth, she kept rubbing her hand over it just to enjoy the feel.

The mail jeep and Mr. Pitt's truck, the only machines she'd ever ridden in, weren't anything like this.

As Gene slid under the wheel, she said, "I'm sorry to stop your work."

"No sweat," he replied, and deftly swung the big car out of the parking lot. "I'm working for Dad this summer, doing research for him. If he tells me to take time off, who am I to argue?" He looked over at her and grinned. "This beats reading law books any time. I'm glad you came by."

She wasn't sure what to say to him, so she sat looking out the window. Seeing the landscape whiz by in a blur still made her dizzy, but the car moved along smoothly and wasn't half as frightening as the truck had been—or else she was getting used to this breakneck speed.

"You get to Burlsville very often?" Gene asked.

He must not realize how funny his question was, she thought. "Law, no! I've never been out of the hollow before. Just to Wells Lick."

"Honest? You mean you found your way to High Street and you've never been farther than that store up in the mountains?"

"Well, I had some help." She explained about the Pitt brothers, then added, "I was scared, and that's the truth. And I still am, seeing so many wondrous strange things I've never seen before."

"Yeah, I guess a lot we take for granted would be new to you," Gene said thoughtfully. "That's fantastic!"

Fair Annie stole a glance at him and found him as handsome as she remembered. She'd prayed for a pretty young man and here he was, right beside her. Yet she didn't think that he was the answer to her prayers. The "chillburnin'" that had run up and down her spine when she'd walked beside him up the mountain road was missing now. It wasn't the same. She suspected that a mountain boy with strange eyes and hacked-off hair had something to do with it.

"Your father said that you're a scholar," Gene commented. "When do you finish high school?"

"I don't know . . . depends on the weather. It's a long walk to school, but I go as often as I can."

"Maybe you'll try college. I just finished my freshman year at Shipton University in Burlsville. It's a pretty good school. You'd like it."

Fair Annie wanted to laugh, the idea was so preposterous. Most of the time, finishing high school seemed an impossible goal. But college! It had never crossed her mind. Besides, lately she'd been giving more thought to marriage than to school.

"I couldn't go. It costs too much money," she said, not really caring, just to make conversation.

"Not necessarily. There are scholarships. If you're interested, Dad might be able to help you get one. He's a trustee of Shipton."

They turned off the highway onto the mountain road that became progressively rougher. Gene drove carefully, trying to avoid the worst ruts.

"I can see why there isn't much traffic up here," he said. "The cars fall apart after one trip."

"I reckon the road people know we aren't going anywhere, so they don't bother to fix it. A lot of folks like it rough because it keeps outsiders out."

"I can believe that!" Gene said with a laugh. "It's enough to discourage all but the brave—like me, sometimes known as Fearless Gene. But even though my bravery knows no bounds, how much farther is it? Seems longer than when Dad was driving up here."

She'd never had anyone joke with her this way and found herself grinning like Otis. "It's not far now. But I could get out and walk from here."

"Nothing doing. Besides, there's no place to turn around."

"This road ends at Wells Lick, where you parked last week. After that, it turkey-tails out into the hollows; and all of them are rough, mostly fit for a mule."

"Good idea! Next time I come, I'll bring a mule and ride right up to your door. Bet you'd be surprised."

They cleared another hill, and the little settlement at the junction of Great Day Creek and Wednesday Fork came into view. Gene pulled up in front of the store.

"Since I don't have a mule, I'll have to stop here."

"My family would be pleased to have you walk up to the cabin," Fair Annie said, hoping that if he accepted the invitation, Patty Ruth Ann wouldn't be there.

Gene shook his head. "I have to get back to work. Dad says this job is a business arrangement, and he's very strict. He'll make me work overtime if I stay away too long."

Fair Annie mentally wrestled with words, trying to find

the right ones to express her gratitude to the Armours. In the end, she could think of nothing better than, "Thank you . . . you and your father. I hope he won't feel too bad if the sheriff won't listen to him. My kin will still be proud that he tried to help."

"Don't write Dad off that easily. If the law's on his side, he won't give up. Course it's harder when politics are mixed in, which is usually the case with the coal companies. But don't start worrying just yet. He may spring your whole tribe."

Before driving off, he put down the window and called to her, "Fair Annie, I'm definitely going shopping for a mule!"

She waved and went into the store. Mr. Wells and a group of elderly men who regularly passed the time there were watching from the window.

"Didn't expect you back so soon," Mr. Wells greeted her. "Did that lawyer man throw you out?"

"No, he was very nice. He's trying to get the men out of jail right now."

"There! What did I tell you, boys? She went right into Burlsville. Mr. Pitt drove her down the road. I asked him to, myself. And she saw that lawyer man what come up here to write down songs. Don't know why he does it, but if he can get all them folks out of jail, I won't ask. Makes no difference to me."

Old Mr. Jones shifted his position on a sack of dried beans and said, "What's hit like down there in that town, Fair Annie? I ain't ever been closer 'n Black Crow Gap.

And that was fur enough! I don't believe God intended us to live all bunched together like that."

"There were more people than I've ever seen!" she replied. "And they have tall buildings—one layer on top of the other like a cake. The lawyer was in one that had six layers. I didn't care for that because you had to go all the way down to the bottom one to get in or out."

The men shook their heads in disapproval over such an arrangement.

"Well, that was a mighty pretty car you came back in. And a mighty handsome feller what drove hit," said Early Taylor. "With all yore schoolin', Fair Annie, you oughta take up with a feller like that. Someone with a eddycation."

"She don't need to go to town to find an eddycated feller," Mr. Jones asserted. "We got one right chere. Accordin' to what I hear tell, one of them wild McFarrs's got a mess of learning'."

They hooted and slapped their thighs as they caught the joke. "Whoo-eee! I kin jes' see old Ned Collins's face if a wild McFarr showed up to court one of his daughters. Why he'd fill him so full of buckshot, he'd look like a sieve."

Fair Annie knew that this was only a chance remark—the McFarrs were often the butt of their jokes—but she felt her ears grow red and she edged toward the door.

Then Early changed the subject and she was grateful. "I reckon that lawyer man'll git them folks out of jail," he said, while he rotated a quid of tobacco over his four widely spaced teeth. "Soon's you git a lawyer, the govermint sets up and takes notice."

"How come the law didn't carry you off, Early?" one of the men asked.

"Same's they didn't git you," Early replied. "They took one look at me and figgered I couldn't make hit to the door, much less up Juniper." He began chuckling. "I tell you, I crept 'round, jes' barely able to move. Course I didn't tell 'em I went huntin' up on that mountain all the time."

Fair Annie left them trying to top each other's stories about how they put one over on the sheriff. She could hear them cackling all the way up the road along Great Day Creek. And her ears still burned.

chapter thirteen

"Hit's about time!" Mollie Vaughn exploded when she saw Fair Annie. "Here we got all the plantin' to do, and you go and hide. I'd give a pretty to know where you been. We looked all over."

"Law! We looked everywhere!" her mother said. In the dimming light, the lines on her face appeared deep as gullies. "I didn't rightly think you'd play us unfair like that, Daughter."

Then Nancy Belle chimed in with her two cents' worth of indignation, and even mild-natured Barbara Allen was annoyed. Fair Annie realized that a hard day in the hillside fields was responsible for their short tempers, but she couldn't help feeling guilty about deserting them.

"I'm sorry, but I thought we ought to try to get the men out of jail. Everybody says you can't deal with the law without a lawyer, so I went to find us one."

"You mean you went lookin' for that Mr. Armour?" Mollie Vaughn asked in disbelief.

Fair Annie nodded. "I found him, too. Told him about the sheriff. He got mad when he heard how they came into the hollow and rounded up the men. He said they were supposed to have some sort of paper . . . a 'warrant,' he called it. Anyway, he went to see about getting the men out."

"You went all the way to Burlsville?" Ma asked. She seemed unable to get beyond this incredible fact.

"Yes, ma'am. And Mr. Armour's going to help," Fair Annie repeated.

But Mollie Vaughn was skeptical. "Outsiders don't go around doing things for nothin', specially lawyer men. What's Mr. Armour goin' to git out of this?"

"Well, he did seem a right upstandin' feller, even if he be a lawyer man," Ma interposed. "Maybe he don't want nary a thing more'n to come back and hear us sing agin."

"I . . . I offered to pay him," Fair Annie admitted. "But he wouldn't accept it. Strip mining makes him boiling mad because it ruins the land, so I think trying to get the men out of jail is his way of fighting the coal company."

"You offered to pay him! Where'd you git money?" Mollie Vaughn demanded.

"Not money, but things that we make . . . quilts and dulcimores . . . Only he pronounces it 'dulcimer.' He said we didn't owe him anything."

"Well, hit don't matter what he calls hit, as long as he can git yore pa and brothers out of jail," Ma said. "I declare, hit don't seem natural without them 'round. And they ain't used to being penned up like that. They need room to move about."

Mollie Vaughn, pacified at last, said, "I'll tell you for true, if he can git our kin free, I'll praise him right highly. And I'll make quilts for him til my fingers give out." She glanced at Barbara Allen, who had turned away to hide the tears streaking her face.

"The law went up the holler and caught some others, including Billy," Mollie Vaughn explained to Fair Annie. "Unless a miracle happens, there won't be a weddin' on Saturday. And Billy'll be in trouble with the govermint if he don't show up for the Army on Monday."

Fair Annie believed that Mr. Armour would do his best, but he'd warned her not to expect miracles. Now that she looked back on it, maybe she shouldn't have expected much at all. That sheriff was tough. It wouldn't be easy to get him to change his mind. Then another doubt set in, one that she tried to ignore because it seemed disloyal to Mr. Armour. But she couldn't help wondering if he'd said he'd help just to get rid of her. Then she was annoyed with herself for being so suspicious.

The long faces around her reflected her own feelings. To cheer up the girls as well as to revive her faith in Mr. Armour, Fair Annie began telling them about her adventures in Burlsville. They all listened attentively as they prepared supper. Barbara Allen was mixing tears with the biscuits, but she perked up at the mention of Gene. She was always on the alert for romance, and she thought she detected it now.

"I think that pretty feller likes you, Fair Annie. Did he say he might come callin'?"

Fair Annie didn't blush this time. She could handle comments about Gene. It was only Dan'el's name that made her self-conscious. "You hear a wedding tune in every song," she reproached her sister. "Gene's nice, and that's a fact, but he probably has more city girls than a dog has fleas. He wouldn't want a hillbilly like me." She paused, reflecting on her trip. "It's different out there . . . nothing like the hollow."

"That's for true!" Mollie Vaughn agreed, although she'd never been "out there" in her life. "Anyhow, you got schoolin' ahead of you, Fair Annie. So don't you go givin' her ideas about city boys, Barbara Allen."

The rain that had been pattering against the windows began in earnest, hammering the tin patches on the roof as it came down in a torrent.

"I knowed hit was a -fixin' to pour," Ma said. "The birds was flyin' low and the clouds was hangin' 'round the sun when hit set—sure signs."

The cabin door opened and Patty Ruth Ann rushed in, dripping wet. Her timing was perfect again, Fair Annie noted. She'd stayed away until the work was finished but had returned just in time for supper.

Her cousin shook the water off her coat and hung it on a

nail beside the door. "It's a drowner, all right! My folks been cleaning the mud out of our house all day, but if this keeps up, the creek'll overflow again, for sure. My brothers were helping, too. The law didn't get them because they were camping out with Tom Wells. They slept through the whole raid. But a lot of others got picked up."

"You had yore supper yet, Patty?" Ma asked.

"No, ma'am. I'd be proud to set down with you."

For the first time that they could remember, Ma offered the blessing. This was Pa's prerogative as head of the table and of the family, and there was never a substitute except when the preacher came to dinner.

Ma raised her bowed head, looking pleased that she'd carried out this ceremony as well as Pa. And like Pa, she decided the topic of conversation.

"Tomorrow we'll plant the patch by the chicken house, and . . ." She got no further. The door swung open and there stood Pa, with her sons pushing in behind him to escape the rain. Their clothes were wringing wet, but that was the least of their concern right now.

"What's eatin' you, Woman?" Pa roared as Ma sat staring at him. "You act like yore seein' a ghost." He was obviously happy, but, in mountain fashion, he covered his emotion with gruffness.

Ma jumped up. "Well, Lordy, I did think I was seein' a ghost! I never thought I'd see the likes of you tonight. And in all this rain!"

Lord Randal, who always came closer to expressing his true feelings, said, "We couldn't wait around for hit to stop. We wanted to git home as fast as we could. After that jail, the holler never looked so good."

As usual, S. William brushed the whole thing off with a joke. "To tell the truth, that jail was so nice, we hated to leave. But we missed yore cookin', girls. Never did taste such a mess as they served up down there."

Ma began rounding up dry clothes, while Mollie Vaughn added wood to the big kitchen stove.

"Git by the fire, or you'll all catch yore death," Ma urged. "Soon's you dry off, I'll git some victuals."

Pa put on a dry shirt and took his place at the head of the table. His sons quickly joined him.

"I warn't certain I'd see the outside of that jail agin," Pa admitted as he shoveled in beans without asking another blessing. "Them lawmen wouldn't listen to nary a thing we had to say."

S. William said, without being asked, "I heard the sheriff tell one of his deputies that the Axel Coal Company was breathin' down his neck right smartly and wantin' him to arrest somebody. He said—and these wuz his very words—'I'm a-goin' to keep them hillbillies locked up tight so's they cain't do no more damage.' That's what he said. Didn't care who was guilty and who was innercent, as long as the coal company didn't complain."

S. William was indignant, but not indignant enough to stop eating. "Plenty of food in jail," he went on, "but nothin' fit fur a mountain man. This shore tastes good!"

"How come they turned you loose?" Mollie Vaughn blurted out. The others were curious to know, also, but, as was customary, they had waited for Pa to tell them in his own good time.

"I don't rightly know," Pa said, willing to overlook this breach of etiquette tonight. "That Mr. Armour showed up at the jail with a stack of papers and a barrel of lawyer talk. Didn't understand a word of hit, and that's a fact. But first thing I knowed, here come the man with the keys and let us out . . . all of us! And there was a whet of us in there. Then Mr. Armour and that son of his loaded us into some square-lookin' cars and carried us back to Wells Lick. I can tell you, them hills was purely a pleasure to see!"

Lord Randal added, "When Pa asked Mr. Armour how come he was doin' this fur us, he said he was jes' returnin' a favor and glad to be of service. I don't know how he knew we wuz in there, but I reckon word spread fast."

Ma and the girls were careful not to glance at Fair Annie. They knew instinctively that this wasn't the time to break the news about her trip. Pa didn't like to be indebted to anyone, and there was no reason to spoil his homecoming by telling him that his daughter had asked an outsider for help.

Nancy Belle cleared her throat as if she might tell; but when Ma gave her a sharp look and Mollie Vaughn delivered a jab to her ribs, she lost interest in speaking at all.

Fair Annie longed to know what had happened to Dan'el but didn't dare ask.

"Yes, sir, that Mr. Armour did a right good job; got us

all out," S. William said. "Collinses . . . a passel of Browns . . . even a wild McFarr."

Fair Annie almost dropped the cracked cup she'd been drying.

Pa was silent for a moment, then said evenly, "There warn't no wild McFarrs in that jail."

S. William appeared uncomfortable contradicting Pa, but he stuck to his statement. "That boy with the fierce-lookin' eyes, Pa; the one that reminded you of a hawk. That was Dan'el McFarr."

"I thought he was Hessy Brown's boy."

S. William chuckled. "I think the Browns thought he belonged to us. But he were a McFarr. He told me so."

"I talked to him a bit, afore I knew who he was," Lord Randal said. "He seemed a right stout feller—fur a McFarr."

Pa considered the matter, then made a surprising pronouncement: "Them McFarrs has never been right before, but they be right now. That strippin's got to stop. But I cain't figger how ary one got caught. The law commonly stays out of Rancey Holler."

"He didn't say how he come to be caught," S. William said. "I asked him, too, but I don't think he ever did tell. Probably ashamed to talk about hit."

Fair Annie felt a great sense of relief. Her family was together again, and Dan'el was free. Mr. Armour had performed a miracle after all. As she finished drying the dishes, she began to plan a quilt—the most beautiful one they'd ever made. Double Wedding Ring, maybe . . . or Jacob's Ladder. The cloth would be hard to come by, but sometimes there were scraps in the barrel of used clothing that a mission sent the church now and then. Last month they'd sent some pretty pieces of cotton.

Pa took down his banjo and Lord Randal got the crow's quill that he used to play the "dulcimore." First they sang a hymn to give thanks for their release and continued with some ballads. Between songs, the men talked about the jail. All three vowed never to be taken unaware by the law again.

As Pa hung up the banjo and declared that it was bedtime, he said, "Now that I think on hit, I ain't seen Blue's Son fur an uncommon long time. You seen him, Fair Annie?"

The question was completely unexpected. "Yes, sir," she replied, and hoped that he didn't ask where.

"Well, he didn't give out no racket when the law come. Leastways I didn't hear him. But that won't happen agin. I aim to git me a whole mess of dawgs, even if hit takes a bit to feed 'em. Next time the law comes sneakin' 'round, hit'll leave quicker'n hit come."

He sat down on the bed to pull off his boots and told her, "Remind me to take notice of Blue's Son tomorry. He might be needin' a tonic or somethin'."

Her heart sank. She didn't want to make Pa angry, even grown men shied away from that, but he certainly wasn't going to jump for joy when she told him where the dog was. And she couldn't tell him less than the truth if he asked. The only solution was to bring Blue's Son home right away. She just hoped that she could figure out some way to do it by tomorrow.

chapter fourteen

Her sisters and Patty Ruth Ann were still asleep when Fair Annie arose. She had to get through her work and retrieve Blue's Son before Pa remembered that he wanted to examine him. As she dressed, she could hear her brothers and father talking in the kitchen. Ma usually waited until they'd finished breakfast before calling the girls.

When she entered the kitchen, the men were eating leftover biscuits fried in grease and drinking large cups of coffee. They seemed in no hurry to get to the fields, but were enjoying their freedom from jail.

"We give our word," Pa was saying, "and a Collins never goes back on his word."

"But they might throw us in jail all over agin, even if they cain't prove we was on Juniper," S. William protested.

Lord Randal took a gulp of coffee and said in his solemn manner, "Pa's right. We have to show up. We told Mr. Armour we'd be there for the court hearin'. What the law did was illegal, to hear him tell hit, and he's goin' to try to git the case throwed out. I think he'll do hit, too. He's right smart, and that's a fact."

Pa sat rubbing his chin. "I been thinkin' 'bout old Josiah Collins lately," he said at last. "He was our ancestor what found this holler—the govermint give hit to him as a reward for fightin' to git us free from that king in England. My ma used to tell me the story of the Revolutionary War, jes' the way she heered hit from her ma. Hit had been passed down by the generations straight from Josiah. Later on, endurin' the War between the States, our ancestors holped free the slaves. Why the Underground Railroad that took 'em North ran right through these hills.

"Then yore grandpa fit that German Kaiser in World War One, and me and my brothers did our part in the next war, tryin' to free the folks Hitler was gonna make slaves. Now that's a heap of fightin' fur freedom that us Collinses has did. But where's our freedom? Here come the coal companies cleanin' off the hills slick as a whistle—actin' ever bit as high and mighty as Hitler, the Kaiser, and that king put together. Not a dime's worth of difference 'tween 'em. But nobody's speakin' up like they did endurin' the wars. Nobody's sayin', 'Now looky here, Mr. Coal Company, that ain't right an' we're gonna set yore breeches on fire if'n you don't straighten up.'

"No, sir! Now the govermint says, 'Go right ahead and holp yoreself, Mr. Coal Company. Mess up their creeks, tear down their houses, and don't pay no mind to them hillbillies; they don't count.' Now somethin's mighty wrong that the govermint kin do that."

He sat back and drained the large cup that had once been white and was now a mottled gray from years of contact with Ma's coffee—a thick, black brew that sat on the back of the stove summer and winter.

Fair Annie had never heard Pa so bitter. Although he had no patience with the government's red tape, his patriotism ran as deep as his love of the hills.

"Well, hit's the onliest govermint we got, and I s'pect it's better'n most," he muttered, as if to make amends for his harsh words. Then he pushed back his chair from the table and stomped out the door. Her brothers removed the grease from their mouths with a swipe of their sleeves and followed Pa to work.

Fair Annie quickly munched a fried biscuit and washed it down with the strong coffee, diluted with canned milk.

After watching her a moment, Ma commented, "Yore in an all-fired hurry to git to work this mornin'." She sat down opposite Fair Annie at the table and said, "Daughter, I want you to tell me true. Patty Ruth Ann says she thinks yore meetin' a feller down by the crick. Now I don't pay much mind to her tales as a common thing, but if there's a young man that wants yore company, why don't you ast him to call the proper way—right up to the door, like yore sisters' young men? Pa's not anxious for you to keep company, I know, but he'd git more riled up if'n he thought you was seein' someone on the sly."

Fair Annie was angry. "Fine guest she is, trying to make trouble! I haven't met anyone down by the creek. But if I did, it wouldn't be any of her business."

"Now, now, don't take on so. Patty Ruth Ann likes to talk, even when she don't have nothin' to say; sort of runs in the Brown clan. Her mother's a Brown, you know. That's what comes of marryin' out of the family."

Ma waited until Fair Annie had pulled on her sweater for protection against the early morning chill, then told her, "Be sure the sow's feedin' all her pigs. Looks like there's a runt in that litter. Couldn't even see hit yesterday." She looked at her daughter thoughtfully. "You'd best find Blue's Son fore yore pa starts astin' more questions 'bout him."

"Yes, ma'am," Fair Annie replied, and left, avoiding her mother's eyes. It was spooky the way Ma found out about things. But she couldn't know where the dog really was. She must just know he hadn't been around.

Still, Fair Annie was worried as she went about her chores. Sooner or later, someone was going to discover that she'd been going into McFarr territory. Then Pa'd make sure she never saw Dan'el again, if she lived to be a hundred. But in spite of the risk, Rancey Hollow continued to draw her like a magnet. She had to go back one more time to get the dog. That was urgent. After that . . . well, she'd think about that tomorrow.

Fair Annie fed the animals in record time, then once again she headed down the slope toward Old Mule Creek—but only after looking around carefully to be sure she wasn't seen. Big-mouthed Patty Ruth Ann was still in the house, and so were Ma and the girls. Pa and the boys were also out of sight, well down the ridge.

Hopping from stone to stone, she leapt up on the old swinging bridge, getting her bare feet wet only once. But that was enough; they felt like ice. The water flowed from high on the mountain and was always cold. She wiped her feet against the great pads of moss that lined the bank and began the long climb up the opposing slope, her gateway to Rancey Hollow.

Each time she entered this virgin forest, she wondered whether she'd be able to find her way without getting hopelessly lost. It never looked the same. The shadows seemed to fall differently, the trees changed places. It wouldn't take much to make her believe, as most of her kinfolk did, that this was an unnatural place . . . full of boogers.

As Fair Annie pushed on, the sound of the mining machinery grew louder. It was a constant din that she'd almost grown accustomed to. She tried to follow the faint path that led to the rocky area where she'd met Dan'el before. She was certain he wouldn't be there today, not if he just got back home from jail last night.

When she reached the rocks, she was wondering whether she'd be able to find the cave on her own. She hadn't had much luck the last time she'd tried. Then she glanced up, and there was Dan'el, standing on a boulder, just as she'd first seen him—black brows, piercing eyes, and all. Now he was a welcome sight.

"I didn't think I'd see this hollow for a good long time," he said, coming down from the rock. "That lawyer, Mr. Armour, told me you went all the way to Burlsville to find him." He looked at her with open admiration. "If I hadn't been out yonder before, I don't know whether I'd have had the courage to go alone, the way you did. I'm mighty thankful to you. I reckon your folks must be right proud of you, too."

She felt embarrassed. She wasn't used to compliments. "To tell the truth, my father and brothers don't know that I went to see the lawyer. And I'm not sure I want them to find out. I don't think Pa'd be pleased. But I'm glad Mr. Armour could get all of you out of jail. Were you the only one from Rancey Hollow?"

Dan'el nodded. "Only one other McFarr's ever been in jail . . ." He stopped abruptly, and she realized that he was referring to his ancestor who'd quarrelled with one of her ancestors and set off the famous feud. Then he went on. "My father was on his way to try to get me out when he stopped at Wells Lick and heard we'd been freed. Good thing, too. If he'd gone to the jail, that sheriff might have locked him up. The Axel Coal Company wants the law to get tough with folks around here, to set an example. They think that'll discourage others from sabotaging their equipment. Of course, the sheriff's only too glad to oblige, because the coal company helped get him elected."

She had followed the boy up the hill, and now he easily located the cave. As they approached it, a floppy-eared dog rushed toward them.

"Blue's Son!" Fair Annie cried. The dog wagged its tail vigorously, then dashed back among the rocks.

"He looks good as new," Dan'el commented. "Old Woman's a mighty fine doctor."

They found the woman sitting outside the cave again.

"I've cleaned up the cabin, and I'll get you moved today," Dan'el told her.

"I'm more'n ready to go," said Old Woman. "The damp worsens my rheumatiz. Even sang ain't been much help. But I shouldn't complain. You younguns has been mighty good to me, and I know the Lord will bless you for hit."

"You've been mighty good to Blue's Son," Fair Annie said. "I'm going to take him off your hands today."

"How about helping me move Old Woman?" Dan'el asked. "Two of us could get her out in a hurry."

Fair Annie had meant to stay only long enough to get the dog. Her father might decide any minute that he wanted to check on Blue's Son. If he couldn't find him, he'd look for her. The dog was usually wherever she was.

Dan'el waited while she debated with herself. "It's all right if you don't want to . . ." he began.

"It isn't that I don't want to," she said quickly. "It's just . . ." She looked at the frail woman and made up her mind. "Maybe I won't be missed for a while."

The boy gave her an understanding look as he tied the rocking chair to his back. After adjusting the ropes, he knelt down and Fair Annie helped Old Woman settle herself in the chair. Then they gathered up the quilt and bundles and began picking their way among the great boulders that surrounded the cave. The dogs scampered about, chasing squirrels and each other, as if they, too, were glad to be moving. Blue's Son seemed to tire easily, but Fair Annie thought that he was strong enough to make the trip home.

Suddenly they heard a loud, crashing sound. The roar of the mining machinery had become so much a part of the background, they ignored it unless there was a noticeable change. Now they turned and looked upward, just as a bulldozer ripped a particularly large oak tree from the soil, roots and all. As it battered its way down the slope, other trees fell before it, until it finally lodged behind a pile of boulders.

The miners paid little attention to the loss. They continued to scrape away tons of earth and toss it down the side of the mountain, where it had already accumulated into a huge mound. A broad, flat cut that looked like the beginning of a highway circled the top of the mountain, exposing the coal. Even from this distance, they could see the thick, black seam nestled against the heart of the mountain.

"There it is," Dan'el said, his voice edged with bitterness, "the prize in their box of Cracker Jacks. They'll burn it and it'll be gone, but those cuts will last forever. They'll make Old Juniper wash away like Green Pine, until it's nothing but a skeleton."

"Hit benasties the mind for true," Old Woman said. "But don't let hit sour yore days. Men what worship nothin' but money will spend eternity fryin' in hell. And that's a fact."

"I wish I could be sure of that," said Dan'el. "But while we're waiting for them to fry, I'm going to do something about all this destruction."

"You're not going to blow up their machinery, are you?" Fair Annie asked anxiously.

"No, nothing like that."

"Good! Because I don't know whether Mr. Armour could get you out of jail again."

The boy waited. "Aren't you going to ask me what I'm going to do?"

"Well, what *are* you planning?" Fair Annie asked immediately.

Old Woman laughed. "You mustn't jump jes' cause he says 'frog.' Be a little contrary. Hit keeps a man from gittin' too proud." She shot Dan'el a glance. "Course you don't have to worry none about the lad, here. Not a mean bone in his body."

Dan'el smiled. "She thought she'd better add that before I walked off and left her."

"Now I know you wouldn't treat Old Woman that a-way. But what's this yore fixin' to do to them miners?"

"Yes! How're you going to make them sorry?" Fair Annie asked.

"All right, I'll tell you. I had a lot of time to think down there in that jail. Nothing else to do." He had to stop talking to give his full attention to balancing the load in his arms and on his back. They had picked up speed as they moved down the steep slope, past great thickets of laurel and rhododendron, and now the rocky soil was giving way to soft, slick bottomland. It would be easy to make a misstep.

"Well, when I began to think about what had happened," Dan'el continued, "I realized that it wouldn't work. Don't know why I didn't see it before . . . standing too close to it, I reckon. Anyway, I could see that destroying machinery wasn't ever going to stop the stripping. The coal companies have so much money, they could go on buying new machines forever. The only way to fight 'em is the same way they fight us—in the courts."

They stopped to rest while he explained. "They have these smart lawyers who know how to use the law to their advantage. They can get anything they want because we don't know the difference. So I'm going to study law. Then I can fight for mountain folks."

Both Old Woman and Fair Annie stared at him as they absorbed this news.

"I don't confidence lawyer men as a rule," Old Woman said, "but I'll be right proud to have you lawyer fur me, Danny Boy. Us highlanders need somebody to stand up fur us . . . twist the tail of them coal companies hard. They've had things their own way too long."

"Well, what do you think about it, Fair Annie?" Dan'el asked when she said nothing.

"I . . . I think right highly of it. It's just a little hard to get used to. You'll have to leave Rancey Hollow, won't you, to go to college and law school?"

"Yes, and I hate that part. But I'll always come back. I couldn't stay away from these hills for very long. Mama wanted me to get more education, and my grandparents offered to help, but I didn't want to leave the hollow. Now I can see that's the only way to save these hills. I'm going to study hard and fast. Then I'll come back and fight for them with law books."

He seemed more relaxed and happy than she'd ever seen him, as if the decision had given him new incentive.

"I know you can do it, Dan'el," Fair Annie said with conviction. He'd be David fighting Goliath, but she didn't have the slightest doubt that he could do whatever he set his mind on.

At the creek, she put down her bundles to help Old Woman out of the chair. Dan'el couldn't risk carrying her across the slippery log that served as a bridge. While they assisted her, Old Woman shuffled across. There were several moments when Fair Annie thought they would all end up in the water, but they finally reached solid ground without mishap. Old Woman gave a loud whoop of triumph and the dogs barked and ki-yied along with her.

The deserted cabin that was to be her home wasn't far from the creek, and they soon had the woman and her few belongings deposited inside.

"Hit's not Possum Gap, but hit's comfor'ble and I thankee kindly for lettin' me rest these old bones here. Mighty kind of you, mighty kind."

"I must get home now," Fair Annie said. "My sister's getting married tomorrow, and there's lots to do. Ma'll be looking for me."

"That's right, you git back afore yore missed," Old Woman said. "There'd be a mort of trouble if yore kin people knew you was here. When there's been bad blood 'tween generations, hit ain't likely to end soon."

"Thanks for taking care of Blue's Son. He looks real fine now." At the mention of his name, the dog looked at her expectantly.

"Hit pleasured me to have him. He's a good dawg. Now you be careful goin' back." She paused, then said wistfully, "Come see Old Woman agin, lass. Hit gits right lonely sometimes."

"I'll try," she promised, although she didn't think that she'd manage it soon. There was already too much curiosity about her absences, and if Dan'el left to go to school . . .

"I'll see you to the ridge," Dan'el said. Before leaving, he turned to Old Woman. "The miners are getting mighty close to Possum Gap, so I'll go there on my way back and pick up the rest of your things."

"I'd dearly love to have 'em," said Old Woman. "And thankee agin. I'm beholden to you for my endurin' life."

Fair Annie called Blue's Son to follow, but the dog had been left behind so often lately, he wasn't convinced he could leave now.

"Seems like he ain't sure where he belongs no more," Old Woman laughed. "Now go on home, blue dog."

With some coaxing from Dan'el and Fair Annie, the dog finally set out behind them. Dan'el carried him across Rancey Creek, but the dog had no trouble making his own way up the slope on the other side.

Dan'el seemed preoccupied. At length he said, "I'm going to write to my grandparents as soon as I tell Pappy about school. I want to get everything settled before I change my mind. It . . . it's going to be pure pain living away from here."

"You'll be busy. The time'll pass quickly," she said, trying not to think about the long years he'd be gone.

They continued the climb in silence, stopping only twice: once when they came upon a deer that stood frozen in front of them for a second, before bounding off with a flash of its white tail; and again, when a skunk took the right-of-way, confident that it wouldn't be challenged. Blue's Son never seemed to learn about skunks and was ready to charge, but they grabbed him just in time.

As they drew near the top of the ridge, Fair Annie felt an overwhelming sadness. It wouldn't be forever, she kept telling herself. He'd come back. But she knew now that the outside world was different. It would change him. The boy who came back might not be the one who'd been guiding her through Rancey Hollow.

They were at the farthest boundary of McFarr land. Dan'el would go no farther, she knew.

Trying overly hard to be casual, he said, "I reckon by the time I see you again, you'll be married and settled down in your own cabin." It seemed to be more of a question than a statement.

"Maybe. Then again, I may never marry."

The boy looked at her, his keen eyes serious now. She wondered how she could ever have thought they were fierce when they were filled with such gentleness.

"I'll write to you, Fair Annie."

"I'll write back . . . whenever I can buy a stamp."

"Then goodbye. Look in on Old Woman if you can get away safely."

They stood there, each reluctant to leave. She knew that she must go. It was dangerous here because she could be seen from the hollow. But still she lingered, trying to delay this final parting.

It was Dan'el who ended it. With a quick movement, he leaned down and kissed her lightly on the lips. Then, without looking back, he headed in the direction of Possum Gap, where the hungry earth machines still gnawed away at the mountain.

chapter fifteen

Fair Annie went cautiously toward home, certain that she could be seen for miles because of the glow inside her. She felt as if a candle were burning within her, making her shine out like a lightning bug. The pain of parting and the sweetness of the kiss had mixed up her emotions so thoroughly that she wanted to laugh and cry at the same time.

Blue's Son had grown bored with the goodbyes and had wandered off. She could hear him heckling something on the other side of Old Mule Creek.

Throwing caution to the winds, she hurried to the

bridge. Not far along the creek bank, she spotted the bright orange cups of wood lilies, blooming in a patch of sunlight, and stopped to gather a great bouquet. The flowers would come in handy as wedding decorations and, perhaps, divert attention from the fact that she'd been gone so long.

She struggled up the opposite slope with her armload of flowers and checked the pigpen before going to the house. She also looked for Patty Ruth Ann, who always seemed to be around at the wrong time recently. There was no sign of her—until she passed the chicken shed and her cousin stepped out. She'd been gathering eggs.

"Well, it's about time you showed up! Your folks are working me to death . . . doing *your* chores!"

Fair Annie glanced at her flowers and started to explain that she'd been picking them, but Patty Ruth Ann cut her short. "It didn't take you that long to pick flowers." She narrowed her eyes in the way that Fair Annie found particularly unpleasant and added, "I found out you still haven't said a word to your pa about going to Baltimore. You promised to ask him."

"I said I'd think about it," Fair Annie said defensively. "Besides, Pa may not want me to go."

"He doesn't care. He said as much. As long as you're going to school, you might as well be there as here. It's one less mouth to feed."

"He never said that!" She was sure Pa didn't feel that way; at least she hoped he didn't. "I'll ask him tomorrow after the wedding—when things settle down." Now that Dan'el was leaving, there was even less reason for her to stay. And since he'd be living outside, she decided that she might as well learn to cope with city life, herself.

"A promise is a promise and you'd better not forget it," said Patty Ruth Ann, "or I might tell your pa something you'll wish I hadn't." Her cat-that-ate-the-canary expression made Fair Annie uneasy.

"There isn't anything you can tell him that he doesn't already know."

"Well, how about this, Miss Smarty? I have it from somebody even you confidence that you've been going on McFarr land. If your pa knew that, you'd have trouble sitting down for a month."

"Who told you such a thing?" Fair Annie demanded.

Patty Ruth Ann looked pleased with her reaction. "I thought that would bring you down from your high horse. Going on McFarr land's no small thing, you know. It could stir up trouble with that bunch again. And it would be all your fault!"

"You're making it up. I don't believe anybody told you that."

The accusation stung, and her cousin lashed out. "Don't you go calling me a liar, Fair Annie Collins! But if I'm lying, then so is your own dear Otis. He's the one told me. He didn't want to, but he let something slip and I wormed it out of him. He swears he saw you on yonder ridge, talking to one of those funny-looking McFarrs. Otis isn't very bright, but he's truthful. I think your father'll believe him." Patty Ruth Ann smiled, confident that she had the advantage now.

Fair Annie was shaken. But she should have expected this. Almost nothing happened in the hollow that a Collins somewhere didn't observe it.

"I'll talk to Pa tomorrow," she said again, not because of the threat, but because Otis's betrayal was the last straw. There was nothing left for her here, not even trust.

Patty Ruth Ann marched into the house looking so smug that Fair Annie wanted to slap her. She wished once again that she didn't need her cousin's help to go to Baltimore, but she had no other way of getting there. Her only consolation was in knowing that Bertha and Flossie were nicer, and they would be in charge.

"Put yore flowers there," Ma said, pointing to a large jar half filled with blossoms. Every jar and crock they owned seemed to be in use as a vase.

"Hit's purely a sight! Like a flower garden," Ma said, glancing around at the colorful display. "Makes the place right pretty. I hope they don't fade endurin' the night, or we'll have to pick more afore the preacher gits here in the morning."

Barbara Allen was standing on a box in the middle of the kitchen, rotating slowly as Mollie Vaughn pinned up the hem of her dress. She was wearing the muslin gown that Ma had worn when she was married. It had been yellow with age when they unpacked it, but a long soaking in suds from homemade lye soap had turned it almost white again.

"That looks straight," Mollie Vaughn said. "Take hit off and I'll sew hit."

Ma removed a large sheet of cake from the oven of the iron stove, and a delicious aroma filled the kitchen. Nancy Belle edged closer, licking her lips.

"Hit's hot," Ma warned. "And don't you dast lick a crumb. Hit's fur the weddin' guests tomorry." She put the cake down to cool. "I reckon we'll have to cut hit into little pieces so's hit'll go 'round." She began sprinkling it with a bit of sugar in place of icing. The taffy for the party had almost exhausted their supply. The coffee served at the wedding would go unsweetened unless someone who was "drawin'" brought along a pound.

"Hit's enough, Ma," Barbara Allen said. "Folks ain't supposed to stuff theirselves at a weddin'."

Her mother searched in a drawer under the table and brought out three small candles. "I saved 'em when the Ladies' Guild had a birthday party for the preacher's wife." She stuck the candles in the center of the cake. "They'll look gaily when we light 'em."

While Mollie Vaughn sewed, she also acted as boss of wedding preparations and kept Patty Ruth Ann and Fair Annie running with last-minute jobs. Although her cousin was an expert at avoiding work, she was no match for Mollie Vaughn, who thwarted all her schemes. Pa and the boys came home in the midst of the activity but quickly left again. They wanted no part of women's work.

It was late afternoon and dusk was darkening into night before Fair Annie found time to feed the animals. She was slopping the pigs when the churchbell suddenly tolled. Ordinarily they couldn't hear the bell, but tonight the weather conditions were just right and the deep, solemn peals resounded in the valley. Fair Annie listened, automatically counting the strokes . . . seventeen, unless she'd missed one.

The ringing of the bell on a weekday meant only one thing: Someone had died. And it must be someone young, because the number of strokes always indicated the person's age. Another Brown, probably. Their children were all accident-prone.

By bedtime, the girls were exhausted. Yet in deference to this special occasion, they obligingly took a turn in the metal washtub. It was only Friday, but it seemed fitting that they should be clean for this milestone in Barbara Allen's life. Even Nancy Belle faced soap and water without the usual hysterics.

Fair Annie omitted her prayers and hoped she wouldn't "fry in hell," the fate Old Woman predicted for sinners. She was too tired to pray—or to think about Dan'el. She wanted to keep her moments with him safely tucked away in the closet of her mind, to bring them out when there was time to relive her memories.

She fell asleep quickly and dreamed that she was getting married. Only no one came to the wedding—not even the groom.

chapter sixteen

The day had been made for a wedding. As soon as the sun dipped into the hollow and dried up the morning mist, the sky became blue and cloudless, the air soft and warm. A stiff breeze threatened to tarnish the scene with dust from the strip mining on Juniper Mountain; but then the wind shifted, and once more the sky was as clear as in the days of Josiah Collins.

The kinfolk began arriving and soon separated into three groups: the women talking woman-talk; the men slipping behind the cabin to sample the hard cider that Grandpa Collins had brought to celebrate the occasion;

and the children, with dire threats for "roughhousing" hanging over them, standing around awkwardly.

At last Reverend Barclay came puffing up the hillside, almost too out of breath to speak. He had known Barbara Allen since she was born and had gone to a great deal of trouble to make this special trip here to marry her. Weddings were usually held on the third Sunday, when he came to Wells Lick to preach. But since Billy was scheduled to go into the Army on Monday, there wasn't time to wait for his regular visit.

The guests crowded into the cabin, and those who couldn't squeeze in stood on the porch and peered through the open door. Reverend Barclay opened his little black book, moved to the center of the room, and led the singing of "Wedlock," an old religious ballad.

When the singing ended, Billy, looking scared and self-conscious, took his place before the preacher. He stood very stiffly—partly out of fright, but mainly because he was wearing his father's blue suit and it was a little snug. In fact, he didn't dare take a deep breath.

There was an expectant silence, then "oh's" and "ah's" as Barbara Allen emerged from the kitchen on Pa's arm. She looked radiantly beautiful in the off-white muslin dress, and Fair Annie thought that she was the loveliest bride the hollow had ever seen. She was proud that she'd had a hand in helping her look that way. She had brushed the long, blonde hair that fell in such pretty waves around her sister's face. And she and Nancy Belle had picked the blue violets she carried. The faded pink ribbon around them was Ma's contribution. Once, long ago, it had decorated a box of candy.

The crush of people in the cabin kept Fair Annie pinned against the wall, and she was glad that the preacher made the ceremony brief. In just a few minutes, it seemed, he uttered the important questions: "Do you, Barbara Allen, take this man . . .?" And "Do you, Billy Salathial, take this woman . . .?" She could scarcely hear the "I do's," but it was over.

Pa took down his banjo, Uncle Druxter tuned up his guitar, and the wedding party moved outside where there was more room to dance. Billy shed his tight coat and seemed more relaxed. With the formalities out of the way, they could all be themselves again.

The men had carried the heavy kitchen table outdoors, and Fair Annie helped Ma arrange the cake and coffee on it. As she glanced around, she saw Otis across the yard watching her. When she caught his eye, he quickly turned away, guilt written all over his face. She decided to let him squirm in uncertainty, not knowing for sure whether she was aware of his betrayal.

When Reverend Barclay came to the table, Ma gave him a piece of cake and a cup of coffee, then thanked him again for "preachin' the marriage."

"Only too glad to do it," he said. "Barbara Allen's just like a daughter. Why I remember the first time I saw her . . . a tiny little thing, but pretty even then."

"Cain't you stay the night with us?" Ma asked. "Hit's a long way back, and we've got room. You can have Lord Randal's bed."

"Thank you kindly, but tomorrow's my Sunday to preach at Jackson Corner. I wouldn't have time to get there from here. And now I'm afraid I have to leave—to do a little more of the Lord's work. Only it's a sad duty this time. Life's certainly full of contrasts. While you're having a happy wedding here, they're mourning over in Rancey Hollow. One of the McFarrs was caught in a landslide below that strip mining. A tragic thing! According to Mr. Wells, the miners piled that overburden on the slope and a hard rain the other night loosened it. When I left my car at Wells Lick today, there were some lawyers in the store, asking directions. I reckon the coal company wants to make sure it isn't blamed. Don't know how they'll manage that, but those lawyers usually find a way."

"I'm right sorry to hear they've had a dyin'," Ma said quietly. "We don't have dealin's with McFarrs, but I don't wish them grief, either. We all have enough as hit is."

"Well, they're strange, it's true, but part of the Lord's flock all the same," said the preacher. "I think they'd like a few words of sympathy and prayers, although they didn't send for me. I don't even know who died. But I'm always glad to serve wherever I can."

Fair Annie hadn't been paying much attention, but as the words slowly registered, an icy finger touched her heart. It couldn't be! It simply couldn't! But the bell had tolled seventeen . . .

S. William and Lord Randal were standing nearby. They might know who it was. Sometimes they found out about things that happened miles away. But what could she ask them without revealing that she knew a McFarr, that she'd actually been in Rancey Hollow? While she hesitated, the boys left. But she had to know. And she could think of only one way to find out.

The dancing and merriment increased right along with traffic to the cider jugs. This was a good time to get away if she was going. Fortunately, all of the activity was concentrated at one side of the cabin, so she might not be noticed.

After looking around for big-mouthed Patty, she spotted her dancing with Otis. They deserved each other, Fair Annie thought. She entered the back door of the empty cabin and went quickly out the front. No one was on the porch, and she had clear sailing as far as the pigpen. If anyone saw her, they'd probably think that she was being extremely conscientious, doing her chores during a wedding party.

From the pigpen, she looked back. The dancing was going strong and would probably last for hours. If she hurried, she'd be back before it ended.

Fair Annie rushed down the slope toward Old Mule Creek, falling in her haste. She got up, wiped off her scratched knees, and went right on. At the creek, she looked up the dirt road and saw the preacher starting down it. She almost tumbled into the water in her haste to scramble across the swinging bridge before he could see her.

He was taking the best route, following Great Day Creek until it joined Rancey. But she didn't dare go into the McFarr hollow so openly. All she wanted to do was reach Old Woman's cabin and find out the answer to the question that was tearing at her insides. By now she had almost convinced herself that she was making this trip for nothing. Dan'el would be amused that she'd been so concerned about him.

Entering McFarr land was the same bewildering experience as before. Each time she was certain that she'd never find her way through the dense, frightening woods. But she'd finally begun to notice familiar signs here and there—a peculiar scar on a tree, an "M" chiseled on a boulder—things that she must have recorded in her subconscious, because she'd scarcely been aware of them.

She pushed on, slipping on sharp rocks and getting more cuts in return, but she ignored the pain. Something was driving her on now, as if her worst fears might be realized if she stopped. She had to get to Old Woman's house quickly.

At last she could see Rancey Creek bubbling below her. It had been clear before the rain. Now it was brown with mud from the mountain's wounds. She must be close to the cabin, she reasoned, but she couldn't be sure whether it was to her right or left. As she descended the slope, she caught sight of a weathered shack around a bend in the creek, not more than a hundred feet or so away. She walked along the creek bank until she reached the house. This was definitely the place they'd cleaned up for Old Woman. Her dogs were on the porch, watching warily. They didn't bark but whined an alarm when she approached.

Old Woman poked her head out the door. As soon as

she saw Fair Annie, she burst into sobs. "I was hopin' you'd come. I didn't know how to git word to you." She sat down in her rocking chair and wiped her eyes on a piece of cloth.

Fair Annie just stood there, staring at her. She had to force herself to speak. "I didn't know . . . Was it really Dan'el?" The answer was obvious even before she asked.

Old Woman nodded. "I wisht I could tell you different, but I cain't. And I'm to blame, jes' as sure as I'm settin' here. You recollect when you and him couldn't carry no more down the hill? Well, Dan'el went up to Possum Gap to git the things we'd left behin'. Meantime, them miners had stuck a great pile of earth and rocks up there . . . jes' dumped it all over the side of old Juniper and let hit build up. I reckon the rain made the pile move, but when hit come down, everythin' come with hit—trees, rocks, everythin'. Dan'el couldn't git out of the way in time, and one of them rocks got him, poor lad. His pappy found him."

Fair Annie felt sick. And a cold, hard lump in her chest made it difficult to breathe. As she listened to Old Woman's story, it gradually became a dream. This hadn't actually happened to anyone she knew. None of it was real.

"He's bein' buried afore long . . . up on the mountain in the McFarr graveyard. The men worked all night makin' a box. I gave 'em my satin to line hit; shiny white, prettiest stuff I ever owned. I was savin' hit for my own burial, but Dan'el deserves hit more." She blew her nose vigorously on the rag. "Them coal people oughta be horse-whipped!"

Fair Annie wanted to console her, but she couldn't speak. The words simply wouldn't come. She left the cabin in a daze as the elderly woman watched her with a worried expression on her face.

The McFarrs wouldn't welcome her, she knew; but she had to go to the funeral, to be there for this last goodbye.

She wandered up the creek bank. She could find her way from here to the cave, she thought, because they'd brought Old Woman down this route. But after that . . .

She crossed Rancey Creek and started walking—for miles and miles, it seemed. Suddenly she was in front of the cave without any clear memory of how she got there. Time and place ran together. She wasn't sure of anything except her grief.

She tried to remember how they'd traveled from the cave to Possum Gap. She recalled catching a glimpse of the McFarr graveyard near Old Woman's ginseng patch. After climbing over the boulders around the cave, she started up the steep slope and hoped that she wasn't too far off course.

For one startling moment, she could see Dan'el up ahead, waiting to help her over a rough spot. But it wasn't Dan'el, only a shadow. The lump in her chest grew bigger.

High above her was Possum Gap and Old Woman's cabin. The mining machinery up there remained silent today; the great shovels were standing idle. That was the least they could do for Dan'el. Now she could see men milling about on the slope, probably the lawyers trying to prove that the stripping was a blessing after all. Anger jarred her into concentrating on where she was going, and she stopped to get her bearings.

It was about here, she decided, that Dan'el had turned to the right to find the ginseng and the graveyard had been in a clearing just beyond. She turned right, into a cove where she finally found the patch. Looking through the trees, she caught sight of people in the distance.

Fair Annie moved to the edge of the clearing where the McFarr tombstones dotted the hillside. How very quiet it was, now that the machinery had stopped. The McFarrs were gathering around a spot not too far away, and she shrank against a tree where she could see but not easily be seen.

This was the first glimpse she'd had of any of the McFarrs except Dan'el, his father, and the other two men who'd appeared at Possum Gap. To her surprise, the wild McFarrs didn't look very wild. They were mostly middle-aged or elderly, a far cry from the fearsome young men in the legends about the clan. But there was no doubt that they were related. The piercing, hawklike eyes looked out of almost every face.

A man sitting on a rock began to sing in a deep, melancholy voice:

"There were ninety and nine that safely lay
In the shelter of the shepherd's fold . . ."

The others joined in, calmly and unemotionally:

"But one was out in the hills away,
Away, away, far out in the hills so cold . . ."

The faces of a few of the women glistened with wetness, but the rest of the mourners appeared unmoved. As the hymn died away, six tall, gaunt men came slowly up the slope, carrying a rough pine coffin on their shoulders. Dan'el's father led the procession, his impassive expression matching the others. But his eyes were still keen and seemed to take in everything at a glance. Fair Annie moved farther back into the shadows.

The sun shone down brightly on the center of the clearing and left a dappled pattern around the edge where it filtered through the trees. When a breeze disturbed the leaves, the pattern changed and a spot of sunlight focused on two figures under a tree on the opposite side of the clearing. Fair Annie recognized S. William and, she was almost certain, Lord Randal. She was amazed to see them here, yet not especially curious as to why they'd come. It didn't matter. Nothing mattered anymore.

The McFarrs continued to sing as the men, using ropes, lowered the pine box into the ground. Just then another figure, a man dressed in black, approached the grave. The singing tapered off as the McFarrs noticed him. Fair Annie saw now that it was Reverend Barclay. He conferred with the pallbearers. They nodded, and he shook hands with Dan'el's father. Then the men stepped back. The preacher laid his hat upon a rock and began to speak:

"I wanted to come to offer my sympathy," he said, his voice booming across the hillside. "I hadn't known it was the boy Dan'el, but I want to reassure his loved ones that he has gone where pain and sorrow are unknown." Several women wiped their eyes, while the men retained their stoic expressions.

The preacher paused, then abandoning his pulpit voice, spoke in a conversational tone: "I met Dan'el McFarr once, and I've never forgotten the meeting . . ." He went on to tell how he'd become lost while looking for the home of a sick church member and accidentally strayed onto McFarr territory. He'd bumped into Dan'el, or Dan'el had found him, he was never sure which. The boy had taken him within sight of the cabin he wanted to visit. Along the way, they'd had an interesting talk, the preacher recalled, and he had found the boy gentle and intelligent.

Fair Annie reached out and claimed the word "gentle" for whatever comfort it could provide. That was the best way to describe Dan'el—the way she wanted to remember him. His eyes were fierce and he carried a rifle, but he was gentle. And kind . . . She wanted to cry, but tears wouldn't come. Instead the lump in her chest grew larger and more painful. She couldn't understand it. When she'd been stung by a wasp, she'd cried. And when the cow stepped on her bare foot, she'd wept buckets. But she could shed no tears for Dan'el.

The preacher said a prayer, and someone started another hymn as the men filled the grave. Then gradually, the McFarrs drifted away to the hidden recesses of the hollow where they lived. Reverend Barclay remained briefly, his head bowed. Then he, too, departed, and only Dan'el's father was left. Fair Annie noted that he was no longer the tall, straight man she'd seen in the woods. Now he was bent over, like a broken arrow.

When the last of his kin was out of sight, the man glanced across the clearing and walked directly toward her. She thought of running but decided against it. She couldn't believe that he meant her harm.

Mr. McFarr stopped opposite her and said, "Come here."

She obeyed, leaving the shelter of the trees to stand before him in the glaring sun. His face, as cragged as the mountains, was sternly solemn.

"Well, Daughter, he's gone," he said simply. The words seemed to cost him great effort.

She didn't know what to say. The lump in her chest swelled and her mouth felt too dry to speak.

He studied her for a minute. "Dan'el told me about you. Said you'd had a right smart amount of schoolin'. He did, too. His mama taught him, and he read books all the time. The books are still there, and you're welcome to use them." He started to leave, then added, "Come anytime you've a mind. Take some of them home for a spell, if you like."

Before she could reply, he turned to go. But at that moment, the machinery on the mountain roared into action and both man and girl froze in shocked silence. The funeral was barely over, yet the machines were back at work, adding a final insult to their victim. As they looked on, one of the orange monsters lumbered over to Old Woman's cabin and, with a casual sweep of its great shovel, sent the house crashing down the side of Juniper Mountain. It was gone as cleanly as if it had never existed. Even the cozy pocket that protected it was being erased.

This was the final blow. Fair Annie felt such a sense of outrage that she was ready to explode. She would have battered the machines with her bare hands if they'd been within range. Mr. McFarr walked slowly away, despair in every movement.

Still seething with anger, Fair Annie stumbled toward the slope. She had to get away—anywhere out of sight and sound of the machines. She hadn't gone far when strong arms steadied her: first on one side, then the other. Her brothers were beside her, giving her support. They didn't ask questions, but she sensed that they understood. In all the years they'd known each other, she'd never felt closer to them than now.

S. William and Lord Randal gently led her toward home, across Buckeye Mountain and down beside Here We Come Branch. This was an easier path, one that she hadn't been aware of. Eventually they entered the head of Old Mule Hollow near Uncle Partee's house.

Although her emotions were still in turmoil, Fair Annie found that her mind seemed unusually clear. As the three of them walked along in silence, her thoughts kept going back to the machines and Dan'el's plan to fight them, not with his hands but with law books. He'd intended to use the law to protect the land the same way the coal companies had used the law to destroy it.

Suddenly she knew exactly what she must do. It came to her in a single flash, as clear-cut and well-formed as if she'd thought about it for months. She would take Dan'el's place. The mountain folks desperately needed a lawyer, and Dan'el had planned to fill that need. Well, now she'd do it. She'd take on Goliath. For the first time, education wasn't something Pa wanted; it was something she needed, something she had to have. And Gene had said that his father could help her get a scholarship.

She stood a little straighter and walked with more assurance. She knew where she was going. Her brothers, noticing the change, let her walk alone.

When they reached home, the first person they saw was Patty Ruth Ann, lugging in an armload of wood for the kitchen stove and looking very unhappy about it.

"Your ma's had supper ready for a good hour! Where've you all been?"

When no one answered, she put down the wood and said to Fair Annie, "When you get to Baltimore, you won't have to do hard work like this. We just turn a knob on the stove if we want to cook."

Her brothers gave her a surprised glance, and Fair Annie knew that they hadn't heard about her cousin's invitation.

"I can't go. There are things I have to do here," she said firmly and with no apologies. The girl could do nothing now to intimidate her.

Patty Ruth Ann glared. "You promised!" Then she tried another tack. "Well I reckon it's my duty to tell your pa you've been going on McFarr land. When he gets through with you, you'll wish you'd gone with me."

S. William took a step forward and said very quietly,

"You hush yore mouth, Patty Ruth Ann! You tell Pa any tales and I'm gonna personally tan yore bottom, jes' like yore folks should of done years ago."

With that, he abruptly went into the house and Lord Randal did the same. Patty Ruth Ann put a hand to her face as if she'd been struck. Neither she nor Fair Annie had ever heard the easygoing S. William speak so sharply.

"What's going on around here, anyway?" Patty Ruth Ann asked; only this time she spoke in a subdued voice, as if afraid that S. William might come back and carry out his threat.

"I'm sorry about Baltimore," Fair Annie told her. "I thought that I wanted to go . . . I really did. But going won't change things, I can see that now."

"What in blue blazes are you talking about?" Patty Ruth Ann's eyes filled with suspicion. "You know, there's something different about you. You even look different."

"I guess I look older. I've grown up a lot today."

Fair Annie headed for the pigpen, leaving her cousin staring after her, open-mouthed.

It was dusk now, with night coming on rapidly. The blue shadows lengthened, and mist drifted down from the mountaintops. The valley was unusually quiet. Even Uncle Druxter had omitted his evening holler. The wretched lump in her chest was still there, giving her no peace.

High up on the mountain, someone plucked a few chords on a guitar and a girl began to sing. The wavering notes grew stronger as they floated down the hollow:

> *"I gave my love a cherry without a stone.*
> *I gave my love . . ."*

Memories of that day on Rancey Creek came back in a rush. She and Dan'el had sung that song as they cleaned the cabin for Old Woman. Tears welled up and splashed down Fair Annie's cheeks. They wouldn't come before; now they wouldn't stop. She leaned against the rough boards of the pigpen and sobbed uncontrollably. If only tears could make things right again.

> *". . . A ring when it's rollin', it has no end.*
> *A baby when it's sleepin' has no cry-en . . ."*

She could weep no more and wiped her eyes on the hem of her dress. Blue's Son licked her hand. She felt drained and empty, but the lump in her chest was smaller. The pain had eased.

Fair Annie watched a curtain of mist descend on the mountains and their bittersweet secrets. Suddenly through the mist, came the tall, lanky boy from Rancey Hollow, striding along a distant ridge. She could see the piercing eyes, feel her hand in his . . . She knew, then, that in these hills, Dan'el would never be far away.